# Lisa Renee Jones

## WATCH ME

**HARLEQUIN**®

entertain, enrich, inspire™

Recycling programs
for this product may
not exist in your area.

ISBN-13: 978-0-373-79714-1

WATCH ME

www.Harlequin.com

**Printed in U.S.A.**

## ABOUT THE AUTHOR

Lisa spends her days writing the dreams playing in her head. Before becoming a writer, Lisa lived the life of a corporate executive, often taking the red-eye flight out of town and flying home for the excitement of a Little League baseball game. Visit Lisa at www.lisareneejones.com.

## Books by Lisa Renee Jones

### HARLEQUIN BLAZE
339—HARD AND FAST
442—LONE STAR SURRENDER
559—HOT TARGET
590—JUMP START*
601—HIGH OCTANE*
614—BREATHLESS DESCENT*

### HARLEQUIN NOCTURNE
THE BEAST WITHIN
BEAST OF DESIRE
BEAST OF DARKNESS

*Texas Hotzone

To get the inside scoop on Harlequin Blaze and its talented writers, be sure to check out blazeauthors.com.

# 1

SCREAMS FILLED THE AIR, jolting Meagan Tippan, the producer of the new dance reality show America's Stepping Up, from a dead sleep to a startled, heart-pounding sitting position. That was about two seconds before the sprinkler system in the restored Victorian beachfront mansion kicked into gear. Meagan arched her back against the icy fingers of wetness that seeped through her thin T-shirt.

The very real possibility of a fire pierced the momentary shock of Meagan's abrupt awakening. Quickly, she shoved away her soaked blankets and darted across the room. There were twelve hopeful dancers in the house who'd come here to chase a dream, not to live a nightmare, and she had to get them, and her crew, to safety.

Flinging open her door, Meagan found Ginger Scott, one of the two choreographers for the show and "House Mom," in the hallway, rushing the six female dancers in the competition down the stairs.

"Is anyone hurt?" Meagan shouted loudly, because

the water seemed to be muffling everything but the panicked voices echoing around her.

"Just scared," Ginger said, shoving a wet mop of blond hair from her face, as Meagan did the same to her light brown hair. "And I don't see a fire. DJ says he doesn't see one downstairs, either." DJ being her twin brother and male counterpart in the house.

"I called 9-1-1," DJ shouted, rushing up to meet them. "Could be electrical though. Big trouble for a house this old."

Right, Meagan thought grimly. Wouldn't that be peachy? After ten weeks spent casting across the country, with one mishap after another—enough to prompt whispers of a "curse" that she'd hoped to put to rest— only to discover they'd also managed to move into a place with electrical problems, and have it catch on fire their first night there.

"Is everyone okay?" came the voice of another male dancer at the bottom of the stairs. "Do you need help?"

"No! Stay where you are," Meagan yelled, taking in water as she spoke. "We don't need help up here, and there is no fire." *That they knew about,* but she didn't say that. She didn't want to freak anyone out any more than they already were.

"Get everyone on the lawn where we can get a head-count," Meagan said, shooing Ginger and DJ down the stairs. The sooner they had this situation under control, the better. Control? After thirty-two years, and her own dance career destroyed by a knee injury, she should know control was a facade. Just when you thought you had it, it slipped away.

Eventually, Meagan finally had all her hot-bodied,

dripping-wet dancers on the front lawn, looking as if they were posing for a kinky spread in an X-rated magazine. She could only imagine editing this segment. Their stationary cameras had no doubt caught everything and the studio execs would *want* this mishap included in behind-the-scenes footage. After all, they'd insisted on broadcasting every other disaster—from falling sets and broken-down buses, to a crazed fan who'd set the hotel lobby on fire.

A thought hit Meagan like a huge brick. Oh, God. It was a very *bad* thought.

Meagan whirled around to face the house, as if it were possessed, glaring at the monster that was about to ruin everything, even her own career. The chance to pitch the idea for this show had come after years of working as the producer for a top news show in Dallas, Texas. Leaving that job on the long shot that this could survive the ratings war had been a big risk. She knew the chips would be stacked against her. Tonight that stack had gotten bigger. Not only were the cameras getting wet, but the house, where they'd intended to spend the next twelve weeks, was being destroyed by the water. And she had enough experience with fickle network executives to know that her show, her darn dream-fulfilling show, was turning into a nightmare that might well be called "cancelled."

And although the top dancer among her contestants was set to win a new car, a studio contract and cash, while the other dancers would earn major industry exposure that could change their lives, she wondered if it would all end tonight.

Meagan tried to comfort herself by recalling the

high-powered panel of judges she'd secured for the live shows—a well-known choreographer, a highly respected casting agent and even a highly acclaimed pop star. Surely, the studio wouldn't want to pay out their contracts and see no real return.

Who was she kidding? Studio executives always leaned toward taking their financial hits and cutting losses. Meagan had to do something to save the house, if she expected to save the show.

Meagan leapt to action, darting toward the house, ignoring shouts of her name. Clearly, there was no fire, only water—lots and lots of destructive water. She burst through the door, and headed straight to the basement through the kitchen. Though she had no real idea how to turn off the sprinklers, flipping the circuit breaker seemed logical, and she remembered seeing it by the washer and dryer.

Sure enough, the breaker was where she thought it was, but any relief she felt at finding it was doused when she realized it was ridiculously high off the ground. Oh yeah, it was high, well above her reach, or any normal human's, for that matter. Resigned to the climb ahead of her, she splashed her way closer.

She couldn't help but ask herself if the night could possibly get any worse, as she heaved herself on top of the washer.

Footsteps sounded on the stairs, and she yelled over her shoulder, "I said go to the lawn!" She jerked the metal panel, but it wouldn't open. "I need everyone outside and safe." There was the sound of more splashing and she grimaced. "I said—"

"Come down from there before you get hurt," came an order from behind her.

Meagan froze at the deeply resonating voice of Samuel Kellar, the sexy, blond-haired, blue-eyed, irritating, arrogant, six-foot-two—if she had to bet her life on it—head of studio security, who she knew all too well and wished she didn't.

Samuel, or Sam as everyone called him, had directly coordinated much of the show's security over the past few months, especially the open casting calls. She'd had innumerable occasions to know with certainty that few people could rattle her nerves the way Sam could. When Sam said jump, people jumped. He didn't *ask* anyone to do anything, he ordered them. And since that trait irritated her to no end, how was it that the man made her want to both yell at him and strip him naked at the same time—she didn't know.

But shouting wasn't her style, nor was sleeping with a man like Sam. She preferred subtle and submissive, to his demanding and arrogant. Unfortunately, Sam wasn't the least bit dissuaded by her sharp-tongued retorts meant to be off-putting. In fact, he infuriatingly seemed to enjoy sparring with her.

And just when Meagan thought Sam's presence ensured that the night really, truly, couldn't get any worse, it did. With frustration, she yanked at the panel door with an unsuccessful jerk that hiked her butt up in the air. Meagan froze, mortified, in the embarrassing position. Sam, her sexy pain-in-the-backside, now had a view of her backside. Because Meagan was pretty sure her skimpy, wet, hot-pink boxers weren't leaving much to the imagination.

SAM KELLAR MIGHT BE former Special Forces, a man of restraint and discipline who considered himself a gentleman, but he was still a man when it came down to it. And the man in him was standing at attention for Meagan's impossibly sexy, heart-shaped butt, despite the cold shower he was enduring. It said a lot about how much he wanted this "taboo" woman. Taboo because they not only worked together, but she chilled him with her ice-princess routine every time the sparks between them got too hot.

"Get down, Meagan," he ordered, having no doubt he would get an argument—prickly arguments were part of her ice-princess routine.

She yanked ineffectively at the panel door. "Not until I turn off the water."

"I'll do that," he promised. "Come down before you—"

She slipped before the words were out and then tried to right herself. He didn't wait to see if she was going to succeed or fail. Sam wrapped his arms around her long, slender legs to make sure she didn't fall.

"Sam!" she objected, pressing her hands to the ceiling, shifting unsteadily to stare down at him. Their eyes locked. Awareness flashed hot and fast between them, a silent understanding that she was half naked and in his arms, and that this wasn't the first time either one of them had thought about such a moment.

"Let go of me," she said, a hint of panic in her voice, the same panic he heard every time their combustible attraction flared to life.

"And let you break your pretty little neck?" he asked. "Not a chance." Not giving her time to object, he slid his hands to her waist and forcefully lifted her down from the washer. Not an easy task from his lower position, and she ended up plastered against him as intimately as those shorts hugged her backside. And oh yeah, the man in him was alert and present all right. He'd wanted this woman too long not to react to having her lush body pressed to his.

"What do you think you're doing?" she demanded. Her hips were melded to his, her hands pressed against his chest—hands he'd often dreamed of having on his chest and all kinds of other places. Sexual awareness had caught them like the water they couldn't escape.

Her nervous energy escalated, just as her temper did, meaning their same routine as always. "Sam, damn it! The house is being destroyed. My career is being destroyed." She squirmed out of his arms, and reluctantly he let her go. "I have to stop the water." She turned back to the washer.

That, he wasn't letting her do. Sam shackled her arm and pulled her around to face him, and she was close, so close he could kiss her, and damn if he didn't want to in a bad way. He would have, too, if not for the fact that she was right—the water needed to be turned off.

"Stubborn woman," he mumbled. "I'll do it. That's why I came down here in the first place. That and I saw you rush into the house, and knew you were up to no good."

Sirens sounded in the distance, and unintentionally, his gaze brushed her very visible, red, puckered nipples beneath the transparent shirt. He didn't like the idea of the entire fire department getting the same view.

"Sam!" she objected, folding her arms over her chest.

He scrubbed a hand over his face, as if he would ever wipe away the image of those perfect breasts. "Sorry," he said, meaning it. He didn't want to make her feel uncomfortable—no, uncomfortable was the last thing he wanted to make Meagan feel. "That wasn't on purpose. It just…happened." He slid out of the rain jacket he'd put on before coming inside and handed it to her. "Put this on," he told her, "before a gaggle of firemen make the same mistake." The idea of that gnawed away at his gut in an unfamiliar, uncomfortable way.

Sam turned away from her, lifting himself on top of the washer and hitting the button to the panel door that Meagan had missed.

She made a surprised sound. "I loosened the door for you."

His lips quirked, but he didn't reply. He so enjoyed how easily he ruffled her feathers, even when he wasn't trying. He cut the breaker to the sprinklers. The water was off. The sound of firemen's voices and loud, heavy footsteps echoed from the floor above.

He eased to the floor, ankle deep in water. Meagan was thankfully well covered in his way-too-big jacket, but there was something intensely erotic about her in something of his that he couldn't dismiss.

She slicked her hair back, drawing it away from her face, a face incredibly appealing without makeup, au naturel. And then they stood there.

Water clung to her thick, dark lashes, framing grass-green eyes that swept over his wet studio T-shirt and returned to his face.

More of that sexual tension zipped between them.

"We need you folks out of here," came a male voice from the stairs, effectively jolting them from the hot little spell spinning around them.

"We're coming," Sam yelled, and then to Meagan, "Better late than never, but had this been a real fire, people could have been hurt. I'll be talking to them about how this happened. In the meantime, one of my guys is already arranging a hotel for everyone." He motioned for her to head upstairs.

A sudden wave of vulnerability washed across her features. "I ah...considering the firemen and your guys and...well, thanks for the jacket. And for turning off the water." And then, when he thought they'd made some progress, she proved him wrong, pursing her lips and adding, "But I was about to turn off the water myself. I had it. I was getting it."

He couldn't stop the corners of his lips from twitching, despite the certainty that a smile—and most certainly the laugh threatening to escape—would only set him up for a battle. "Of course you would have," he agreed, playing the cat-and-mouse game she seemed to want him to play—though, damn if he knew who was the cat and who was the mouse half the time. "But I'm here, Meagan. Why not use me?"

Her lips parted slightly at the words. Then her brows knit together, and her hands went to her hips, giving him a delectable glimpse of skin below her breasts. "You're impossible," she announced, glowering, before sloshing toward the stairs.

He stood watching her, thinking that the real "impossible" here, was not him, but that either of them believed they were going to be satisfied with this game much longer. She wanted him. He wanted her. And he was going to do something about it. No matter how many washers he had to climb.

# 2

SEEING SAM AGAIN SO SOON after…well, he'd seen her up close and personal wasn't something Meagan welcomed. Not even after she'd had access to a hotel bed for a few hours, staring at the ceiling, thinking about his body pressed to hers.

Now dressed in her conservative black skirt and blouse, feeling a mess, as she stepped off the elevator and directly into the studio's executive offices, she was pretty darn sure she wasn't going to escape Sam's presence. Because instantly, as if she had some cosmic radar for the man, a flutter of anticipatory butterflies overtook her stomach. The kind a lover felt for a lover.

Meagan didn't want to react like this to Sam. Life had taught her not to date men like Sam, certainly not to invite them into her bed. She stuck with the easy-going types, who'd actually listen to what pleased a woman, rather than assuming they knew and getting it wrong. Men who cared about what a woman wanted, which right now, for her, was to keep her job. Scratch that. This wasn't about a job. It was about a dream, about the career as a dancer never realized. About how she could use that passion in a positive way and help others who loved dance. Exactly like a very special teacher had done for her once when she was a young girl working hard to become a top-class ballerina.

With an intake of breath, she reminded herself she was here to pitch shooting the show from the hotel she and the cast and crew had moved into. As far as ideas went, it was a good one. Meagan approached the secretary, June, who smiled her usual friendly welcome from behind an oversize mahogany desk.

"Morning, Meagan. Or maybe not. I hear you had a rough night."

"What doesn't kill you makes interesting television," Meagan replied lightly, shoving a lock of brown hair behind her ear.

June chuckled at her quip. "I'll let Sabrina know you're here."

A masculine voice rumbled behind Meagan, thick with a sensual taunt. "Good morning, ice princess. How are you feeling today?"

Meagan tensed, hating when he called her that, and he did it often. Hating it even more since Sam's presence most likely meant the studio intended to shut down the show. He'd be called in to plan damage control in case of any trouble that might occur when the contestants heard they were headed home.

Feeling nauseous at the thought, she told herself to hold it together, to give him the sass he expected from her. She turned to face him, but found herself captured by his amused, piercing blue eyes that not only sent a sizzle down her spine, but to other more intimate places. And that made the "sass" come a wee bit easier.

"I'm feeling downright chilly, why thank you," she replied, pivoting on her heels and making a beeline for the lobby chairs. She was all too eager to escape Sam's assessing stare. He would see that she wasn't feeling chilly at all—she was feeling hot enough to fan herself. And stare he did, indeed. Settling into one of the black leather chairs lining the wall, Meagan didn't have to look up to know Sam was watching her. She felt his gaze, hot and heavy, following her movements.

Crossing her legs, she snagged a magazine, and tried to live up to the "ice princess" label, rather than the "wanton vixen," that he made her want to be. Despite her effort to resist, her gaze lifted at his approach, tracking the strut that she could tell came natural to him. Meagan's mouth went dry at the sexy way his jeans molded those really nice, strong legs, and at the memory of another pair of jeans, wet and plastered to lithe muscle.

"You're easily agitated this morning," he commented, claiming the chair directly across from her. "I usually have to work harder to get you this riled up."

"I'll just have to sleep less more often," she replied. "Then you'll have your princess raring to go."

He grinned, his eyes twinkling again. "I'm not even going to take advantage of that poorly worded rebuttal because you *are* tired, and I'm afraid you might hurt me in front of Sabrina."

Her cheeks heated as the double meaning of his statement sank in, but before she could reply, the door to her boss's office opened. Sabrina stepped into view, her long blond hair neatly pinned at the back of her neck, her white suit impeccable. "Come in, you two. So sorry I'm running late. Would either of you like coffee?"

"No coffee for me," Sam answered, as he pushed to his feet.

"I'd love some coffee," she said, mostly to contradict Sam, desperate to feel like she still had some semblance of control. It was silly, ridiculous, immature, and proof that she, in fact, had absolutely no control when it came to this man.

Sam arched an eyebrow at her, a knowing look in his too-blue eyes that said he knew exactly what she was thinking. She grimaced. "I haven't slept. Who doesn't want coffee when they haven't slept?" She lifted her chin, and headed toward the office.

Once inside, Sabrina motioned to a small conference table, and Meagan found herself seated between her boss and Sam. A cup of coffee quickly appeared in front of her.

Sabrina flattened her hands on the table. "Well. Where do we begin? We knew this show would be a bit of a crazy ride, but just how crazy were we thinking? The good news is, a crazy ride will usually translate to high ratings. Several of the big gossip websites not only reported last night's occurrence, they're feeding the rumor of the show's curse. Twitter and Facebook are buzzing. So we'll go with this and feed the curse, so to speak. The plan is that over the next two weeks, we're going to show reruns of the auditions. Which gives you that two weeks as a reprieve to get settled in a new house. We'll also run a series of promotional commercials playing up the curse. You'll be responsible for the promotional footage, Meagan. We want to give the viewers glimpses of contestants talking about what happened last night, laced with some spooky 'what if' kind of paranormal flavor. Then play up the curse during the first two episodes. We'll talk from there based on ratings. Everyone will be paid as if on-air for these two weeks off."

Meagan's head was swimming with a mixture of relief and panic. They weren't cancelled. That was good and she'd been in television long enough to understand about working the ratings. "I'm concerned about fitting the dancing in with the curse footage."

Sabrina smiled. "You get two hours for your first episode. Deliver the ratings, and that's just the beginning. We keep the same standard format we've planned all along. One night of reality television. One night of competition and results, with the three judges choosing who goes home. The final show will still be open to votes from viewers. And those superstar performers you wanted us to deliver for the live episodes? That will be your reward if the curse promotionals deliver the viewer interest we believe they will. We'll keep investing in you, and the show, as long as the ratings justify it."

Meagan could hardly believe it. In the midst of a dark disaster, everything was looking really quite spectacular. "That's amazing, Sabrina. I'm speechless," she said. "I won't let you down."

"I know you won't," she said. "Exactly why I support this venture so completely. But everyone isn't as onboard here at the studio as I am. There are liability issues with the situations we've encountered. That means, we have to take some precautions to protect everyone. You and Sam will work together to locate a new house for the filming, and get the contestants safely settled. And then as a final precaution, we'll have on-site, around-the-clock security."

A sudden rush of anxiety came over Meagan, and her heart galloped. Her gaze met Sam's. "What exactly does that mean? Around-the-clock security?"

"It means," Sabrina said, "that this show has big potential, but as things have progressed, it has also proven to have huge potential liability associated with it. The studio prefers to protect the up side and limit the down side of the show. Sam was nearby when he got the emergency call to go to your aid. Next time, we might not be that lucky. In other words, we've asked Sam to handle the show's security with a personal touch, rather than a distant supervisory one, as he has up to this point."

The corners of his mouth twitched slightly. "I'm your new roommate. I'm moving into the house with you."

Meagan's silent gasp delivered a smile to Sam's face. "Am I that bad?"

"There is nothing bad about any of this," Sabrina told them, getting to her feet. "You two are going to make great ratings magic together."

# 3

Meeting over, Sam followed Meagan into the elevator, and the instant the doors shut, she turned to him. "You're the head of studio security. Surely you have better things to do than babysit me and my dancers."

He arched a brow. "That eager to get rid of me, are you?"

"The only thing great we do together is fight."

"I guess it's time we discover what else we do great together," he said, leaning back to study her. "This wasn't my decision, nor was it negotiable. If I hadn't stepped up to the plate and assured the studio I'd contain liability while you focused on ratings, there wouldn't be a show at all. And no matter how big a jerk you think I am, I wasn't going to see you fail, along with everyone else associated with the show, when I could prevent it."

She deflated instantly, her hand pressing to her stomach. "I knew they were going to cancel us."

"But they didn't," he said. "You have a lifeline. We have a lifeline. Which means—" The elevator door opened, and several people were waiting to enter. "Let's talk about this outside."

She inhaled and nodded, and they exited the elevator. The minute Sam was in the lobby, one of his staff rushed into his path.

"Just the man I was looking for," Josh Strong said. A twenty-eight-year-old former navy SEAL who'd gone civilian to care for a sick mother, Josh never missed a beat. Sam was damn lucky to have hired the man. "I've compiled that list of properties you wanted, as potentials for the dance show."

Sam intended to involve Meagan in the conversation, but he was too late. She was already gone, on the move, speeding away from him so fast that she was leaving a trail of smoke.

"Hold on to those for a few minutes," Sam said. "I'll catch up with you." He headed for Meagan with fire in his step. Avoiding him wasn't an option if they were going to make this work, and he was done with the tiptoeing around what was between them anyway.

Sam caught up with Meagan in the parking lot, just in time to press his hand to the door of her Acura, and keep her from opening it. The wind shifted, light brown strands of vanilla-and-honey-scented hair brushing his cheek, his groin tightened uncomfortably.

"We need to talk, Meagan," he insisted.

"Sam," she ground out, tilting her chin up, bringing that kissable mouth inches from his. "Don't hold my door like I'm your captive. And yes, we need to talk, but not now. I have to get back to the hotel and edit film and check on my dancers. And just so we're straight—

you don't get to decide when we talk or do anything. You ask, and we discuss and decide together. Got it?"

Oh yeah, he got it all right. "It" being a rush of pure male need. "Have dinner with me tonight."

"That doesn't sound like a question," she rebutted.

"And if it had been a question, would you have said yes?"

She hesitated, her lashes lowering and then lifting, defiance glinting in her eyes, as she replied, "No."

He didn't miss the hesitation, or the fact that she hadn't complained about his nearness—so close he could lean in and touch her as he had the night before. And he wanted to. Oh yeah, he wanted to in a bad way.

"What if I said I'm bringing the real-estate listings for the housing options?"

"That's bribery," she said. "You could email me the listings."

The truth was, with their limited timeframe, he wanted to review the properties and narrow the list right away, but he didn't tell her that. "Guilty as charged," he agreed and pushed off the car, but he held his position close to her, soaking in the heat of her body, the scent of her hair still teasing his nostrils. "We need to have this talk. Make a truce and set some boundaries, so we can make those great ratings that you want to happen."

"Fine, then," she agreed. "Dinner will include a lesson on the difference between a question and an order."

He laughed. "Fair enough." He loved the way this woman kept him on his toes.

Her expression softened. "I do appreciate you saving the show, Sam."

"Two thank yous in a matter of hours," he said. "I do believe we're making progress."

"Short lived if you forget that I'm in control of my set, Sam, for even one moment. If you want to make changes to procedures, or anything else, you come to me. You talk to me. Then we make changes."

"Understood," he said willingly. "With the exception of anything I see as an immediate threat to someone's safety."

She inclined her head. "I can live with that."

They gazed at each other, electricity sparking in the air. Sam leaned in, lowered his head intimately, to softly say, "I expect you'll be surprised just how much greatness we have between us," he said, and then he pulled back before he did something crazy and kissed her in public. Surely doing so would get him a great big smack in the face. "I'll see you at seven." He turned and sauntered back toward the building, feeling her eyes on him.

"Sam," she called. "Make that seven-fifteen."

He laughed and waved in agreement. She was letting him know nothing with her would come easily. She remained a challenge—but then anything worth having was a challenge. And Meagan was one of the most interesting, impossible-to-resist challenges he'd ever encountered.

He headed back to the offices, only to find Sabrina walking toward him, her purse and her keys in hand.

"I've debated telling you something," she said, "and I don't want it to get out."

"I'm listening."

"When the higher-ups green-lit Meagan's show, they

insisted on attaching a few people to it. One of them was Kiki Reynolds. You might want to keep an eye on her."

"Could she be a real problem?"

"Could be."

Sam nodded, grateful for the tip, and he and Sabrina parted ways.

It seemed Meagan was going to be fighting a whole lot more than her attraction to him in the next few months and Sam vowed he'd be by her side every step of the way.

# 4

SAM KELLAR WAS MEAGAN'S nemesis, proven once again by the fact that she was thinking about *him* rather than the on-camera contestant interviews she was supervising. She pressed her hands into her temples. She still wore her skirt, though she'd managed to trade her heels for flats, she hadn't made time to change, but she seemed to have plenty of time to think about things she shouldn't be thinking about. Sam and his too-blue eyes and his hard, tempting body.

She didn't want to work with him, and she absolutely didn't want to live with him for the duration of the show. That was too close for comfort. She knew darn good and well that if she had even a moment of weakness, Sam would take over her bed, and her life would follow.

She focused on the lounge area of the show's private hotel floor, now newly converted into their interview set. The studio wanted drama, so she was working on giving them drama. She was the producer and mastermind of the show, and should have had a say in Sam's involvement in the show. Still, they weren't cancelled.

Her dream of this program's success, and these dancers' dreams of exciting careers, were still alive. That was what counted.

Derek Rogers, the show's young, hot host, was busy interviewing one of the last female dancers. They were finally about to wrap for the night, which meant Meagan would soon meet Sam for dinner.

Maybe she'd get the male dancers on set for interviews, instead of tomorrow as planned, and just skip dinner. And she really did need to squeeze in some footage of Ginger and DJ talking about the events of the night before. They were, after all, not only choreographing the contestants' routines, but helping to supervise the contestants.

"What were you thinking when the fire alarm went off?" Derek asked Tabitha Ready, who at twenty-eight, was the oldest female dancer competing. Many of the other contestants looked up to her. She was a pretty brunette with loads of talent. She was also an absolute drama queen who was so paranoid about, well, everything, that she seemed better suited as a cast member of Scream than of a dance show. And she was making some of the girls act the same way.

In response to the question, Tabitha seemed to sink deeper in the leather chair she occupied, crossing her arms in front of her pink sweat jacket. "I just knew we were all going to die. We keep having these things happen on the set and I... Just thank God, Jensen was there." Jensen being the male dancer who clearly had a crush on Tabitha. The public was going to eat this up.

Derek, looking every bit the handsome model even in his jeans and *Stepping Up* T-shirt, cast a discreet glance at Meagan that said he, too, believed, this footage was a ratings grabber.

"Jensen carried you out of the house, I understand," Derek prodded, urging her to continue on this path of conversation.

"Oh yes!" she said. "It was horrible. We didn't see fire, but we could smell smoke. We knew any second everything would just blow up." She lowered her voice. "You know. We have a curse on the set."

Meagan cringed every time the word *curse* came up, despite the studio's explicit instructions to play it up. She'd planned for drama to unfold in the house with the dancers—in fact, that concept had been pitched with the show—so one would think a curse would excite Meagan as much as it did the studio, but it didn't. A curse was something that would mess with the dancers' heads and their performances. And ultimately, the dancing had to win the public's hearts. But "the curse" had been given new life and new breath by the house fire, exciting the executives with the promise of ratings. Sure enough, every single dancer had brought it up in their interview. Tabitha, however, seemed determined to own the curse.

"We're afraid of what will happen next," she said. "None of us are going to sleep tonight. I don't know how we'll dance under such circumstances."

The cameraman zoomed in on Derek's deadpan look before he said, "Then you know what you should do?"

Meagan exchanged a "here it comes" look with Shayla White, the director, who was fast becoming a close friend. Hiring Derek, an ex-pro quarterback and sportscaster, for a dance show had been a risk, especially considering he'd lived up to his reputation for saying whatever came to mind. If *Stepping Up* was to succeed where other dance shows had failed, it meant they needed originality, and Derek was nothing if not that.

Derek continued, "Get a lucky charm like us athletes do. In my case, I'd get a pair of lucky briefs."

"Briefs?" Tabitha asked, skeptically. "Eww."

Derek grinned and held up his hands. "Hey, don't tell me you haven't got a pair of lucky underwear."

It took a second but finally Tabitha, and everyone else on set burst into laughter. "Well, maybe I do," she said, clearly giving it some serious thought.

Derek assured her, "At least five guys on my NFL team had 'game day' lucky boxers. They swore they'd screw up on the field without them. They believed those transformed them into men of steel, and so they did." He tapped his forehead. "It's all in your head. It's what you believe."

Tabitha smiled slyly. "And if I don't wear underwear?"

If Derek caught her flirty remarks, and he was a smart guy so surely he had, he didn't show it, nor did he miss a beat. "Socks. They're the next best thing." The entire crew erupted in laughter, and Meagan could just imagine the audience doing the same thing. "But really, Tabitha, whatever works for you. Just make sure that your lucky charm is something you can always have with you. Heck, I knew a guy who had to kiss his wife right before the game or he messed up every play he was in. When she didn't travel with him, he was worthless."

"So maybe I should kiss Jensen." Tabitha beamed.

"Then what happens when one of you gets sent home?"

The air seemed to crackle, the silence thick. It was a brilliant moment that had evolved from a talk of curse, and shown human vulnerability that every viewer could relate to on some level. Tabitha seemed devastated. But it was short-lived. She recovered promptly, showing herself to be a pro at flirtation. "Then maybe *you* should be my lucky charm."

Derek grinned and gave her his cheek, tapping it with his finger. She kissed him, and the crew all broke out in grins.

A few questions later, the interview ended. And just when Meagan thought she'd wrap the night's shooting with a laugh rather than with the curse, Tabitha walked to the edge of the set and went tumbling forward, smack onto her face.

At 6:45 p.m., thirty minutes before his dinner with Meagan, Sam completed his check-in at the hotel, sliding a healthy tip, compliments of the studio, into the doorman's hand to ensure his bag was delivered to his room for him. With way too much eagerness in his step to suit him—considering Sam knew it had nothing to do with duty, and everything to do with seeing Meagan—Sam headed toward the bank of elevators, rather than the restaurant. He knew Meagan wouldn't be there, and he had no intention of sitting around and waiting for her. Not when he'd bet money on her being intentionally late, and then claiming work as an excuse.

It was a control thing to her—her desire to have it and keep it from him. Fine by him. This was her show, and she was in charge and deserved that respect. But as the person in charge of safety, he'd need to ensure he never ran the risk of jeopardizing his authority and ability to do his job in the face of any threat.

So he and Meagan had some hashing out to do. Tonight. Alone. Still, he'd promised himself he wouldn't touch her for all kinds of reasons. Work wasn't the place to play. Smart people knew that bedroom games, and even simple romantic notions, could easily turn emotional and explode, no matter how covertly they began. He didn't do complicated relationships. He did the uncomplicated, casual type. Namely because he'd seen far too many divorces, and tormented, worried spouses like his mother, when he'd been in the army.

Despite all these brilliant assessments about what he had going on, or rather not going on with Meagan, Sam couldn't stop thinking about her. That had never happened to him with a woman before. And as he punched in the code for the private floor the studio had rented for the show, there was no mistaking the thrum of anticipation he felt during the twenty-floor ride, at seeing her again. A thrum he recognized could lead him to trouble. Big damn trouble.

The elevator dinged, and the doors began to slide open. In the same instant, a scream filled the air. Instinct sent Sam into action, darting out of the elevator to draw up short when he found a studio set almost directly off the elevator in the center of a large lounge area. One of the contestants, Tabitha, was lying flat on her face, her mouth bloody. Meagan was squatting next to her. Hovering above her were the twins, Ginger and DJ, who clearly wanted to help the situation, and didn't know how. Kiki, the thirtysomething attractive redhead, stood in the background looking amused.

Sam grimaced at her behavior and headed for Meagan. "Does she need an ambulance?"

"Yes!" Tabitha screamed. "Yes, I need an ambulance. My front tooth is missing! *My tooth* is gone!"

"I called 9-1-1," one of the crew shouted.

Relief washed over Sam. A tooth he could deal with. No one died from a lost tooth. But any relief he felt vanished when the cast of contestants emerged like a pack of wild animals onto the set, as a rumble of questions and panic erupted. The cameras continued to roll, panning the crowded lounge.

Sam's gaze found Meagan's, even as she helped Tabitha to her feet, a silent question in his stare. He didn't want to screw up footage she needed for the show, but they didn't need another injury, either. Fortunately, as usual, he read her easily—the look on her face said *Please get them under control.* The fact that they communicated without words was a testament to the natural connection they shared. That he agreed with her decision, that she confirmed what he knew already—that she wasn't like the studio executives who put ratings above all else—were just more reasons why he wanted to be alone with her.

"Enough," he called out to the group, holding up his hands. "My name is Sam Kellar, and I'm the head of—"

"It's the curse!" Tabitha shouted. "It's the curse."

Screams erupted from the dancers. Sam and Meagan shared an exasperated look before, together, they went into damage control.

The studio wanted footage that fed the curse, and

now, they were sure getting it, but not because he, or Meagan, were trying to deliver it. He and Meagan were just trying to survive and doing so *together*. Oh yeah, staying hands-off with Meagan was going to be about as easy as calming this group down. And that, it appeared, was damn near impossible.

FIFTEEN MINUTES LATER, EMS was gone and Sam and Meagan had agreed that Tabitha should go to the hospital, with one of Sam's men escorting her to avoid the tabloid photographers.

His man, Josh, had just learned he would be that lucky man. "Josh's an ex-SEAL," he explained to Meagan. "If he can't handle Tabitha, nobody can."

Meagan snorted. "Neither of you know Tabitha or you might reconsider that statement. I can't possibly let you take on this job by yourself. Believe me, you'll want backup." Before Sam could object, Meagan flagged Kiki over, and Sam didn't miss the flash of interest across Josh's face.

Sam leaned close to Josh. "I hear she killed her last lover."

Josh, who had a way with the women, said, "I can think of worse ways to die."

Kiki joined them, looking irritated at having been summoned. "I need you to please go with Tabitha to the hospital," Meagan said and pointed at Josh. "This is Josh Strong, one of Sam's men. He'll go along with you for security reasons."

Kiki looked disgusted. "Why is this my job?"

Sam arched a brow at Kiki's blatant disrespect toward Meagan. It heightened his worries about Kiki, but

Meagan responded with remarkable composure. "Because I need to review property options for the show with Sam, and I can't risk any exposure, tabloid or otherwise, that might hurt us. In other words, I need you, my next-in-charge, who has pull and power. Josh here will offer muscle if you run into trouble. You deal with Tabitha and her injury."

"Shouldn't I be included in the property search?" Kiki asked, sounding a bit like a spoiled brat afraid of getting one less cookie from the jar, and not at all concerned about Tabitha.

"When I know where we stand, you will be," Meagan assured her. "But right now, I need you to attend to Tabitha. Go, please."

Kiki frowned and eyed Josh, motioning to her left. "This way."

"Nothing like having a studio exec's niece forced on you," Sam said, imagining that Kiki resented having to work under Meagan.

Meagan turned to him. "How'd you know that?"

"I make it a point to know things," he said. "And I'd watch my back with her. If a curse exists, it's probably down to her. The last three shows she's been on failed."

"Yeah, I know," Meagan said. "I've heard all kinds of rumors about her that I've tried to tune out. I want to give her the benefit of the doubt because I know how gossip grows. And really, it doesn't matter anyway. She's a mandatory part of this show, per my contract with the studio."

Sam wasn't going to tell Meagan everything he knew about Kiki, but he did want to alert her to keep up her guard. "I understand your position, but there is some truth to what you've probably heard. For instance, she did sleep with that producer who ended up fired."

She laughed. "Well, I won't be an easy target in that department, at least. She can't get me into bed to manipulate me. You might want to warn your man, Josh, though."

"I plan to."

She nodded. "Good, because I'd hate to see him hurt when he's just trying to keep us all safe. All I can say is thank God my director is an angel, so I have someone I can truly trust. She was picked for me, too, and she's marvelous."

Meagan could trust him, as well, but he knew she wasn't ready to embrace that concept. Not now. But he intended to change that.

Fifteen minutes later, the contestants had returned to their rooms, and he'd ordered three more security personnel to keep them that way. The crew, who'd been put up in the hotel for ease of filming, headed to the lobby bar to "analyze" the day's events over drinks and food.

Derek lingered with Sam and Meagan. "What about you two? Surely you both need a good, stiff drink or two, after that disaster. And here I thought football players were rowdy. Those kids are crazy."

"You can't say I didn't warn you before you took the job," Meagan reminded him.

Derek scrubbed his jaw. "Yeah, yeah. I thought you were exaggerating." He gave her a pointed look. "You weren't."

"Nope," she said. "I wasn't. So have a drink for me as well because I need one but don't dare indulge. I have work left to do."

Derek eyed Sam and Sam held up a hand. "I never drink on duty, and the next few weeks are all duty for me." Sam liked Derek. Derek had spent his NFL days racking up awards—not scandal—which was exactly why he didn't think Derek would survive beyond season one.

Derek smiled warmly. "All right, then. I'll make an exception to my one drink rule, and have a few for the two of you." He waved goodbye, and trailed after the crew.

Sam's gaze shifted to Meagan to find her frowning. "I so wish this night was over," she pleaded.

"Not yet." He watched her frown, noting the dark smudges under her eyes, half moons on pale perfect skin. "You look exhausted, Meagan."

"Gee thanks, Sam. Just what a girl wants to hear."

"You still look gorgeous," he said, meaning it. "Just tired."

"Compliments delivered after an insult are meaningless and even less effective when followed by 'just tired.'"

"Saying you look tired isn't an insult. It's a concerned observation. I should feed you and review these prospective house locations for you so you can get some rest. My crew will keep an eye on things."

She opened her mouth, clearly intending to argue and then seemed to change her mind. "You and your crew haven't had any rest, either. Last night was hell for us all." She settled her hands to her slim hips and sighed. "I guess we should at least try to eat before someone's screaming about the curse again."

For a split second, he'd seen a softer side of Meagan.

The one he knew she hid behind. He wanted to know more about that part of her.

They stepped into the elevator, neither spoke. Each of them leaned against a wall so that they faced one another. There was no mistaking the way an awareness filled the space. It may be only dinner, but he wasn't leaving that "trouble" he was worried about behind—Meagan *was* trouble. And standing in this car, with the soft female scent of her tickling his nostrils, her green eyes flickering, he wasn't sure it was trouble he could walk away from.

# 5

AVOIDING THE HOTEL'S packed restaurant had seemed a smart move at the time, but she wasn't so sure anymore. While sitting in a dark, secluded corner of the hole-in-the-wall Chinese restaurant next door, Meagan had never been so aware of Sam, never so certain she was captive to her desire for this damnable, impossible-to-ignore man.

His gaze met hers over the menu.

"I haven't had good Chinese in forever." He spoke softly, but everything in his voice, said, *I haven't had you and I want you,* instead. Or maybe she was imagining the hidden meaning, maybe some part of her wanted that to be the case. Because as much as she wanted to hate Sam, wanted to believe there was nothing beyond his arrogance, but trouble, there *was* more there, more to him, more to what she felt for him. It had occurred to her during Tabitha's crisis. He'd not only respected her on the set tonight, but also willingly, efficiently, helped her deal with that mini-disaster.

Suddenly, she noticed she was staring at him—

studying the solid square strength of his jaw, the high cheekbones, the full lips—and not discreetly. His face was as chiseled and perfect as his body.

She cut her gaze to the menu, ignoring his keen stare. "I order from a place near my apartment at least once a week," she said, cursing herself for revealing even one small personal detail. There was just something so darn intimate about the quiet setting, about what felt more like a date than a business meeting, that she welcomed the waiter's interruption to take their orders. Why could she not stop thinking about being in the basement the night before—just she and Sam—both of them wet, her nearly naked, and then wearing his coat? But she knew. It wasn't just the attraction between them that had gotten to her. It was the way he'd been protective, the way he'd helped her. He made her want to hand him just a little control, and that frightened her. She'd dared to do that a few times in her life and each time had led her to the wrong place.

They placed their orders, the silent awareness springing back into place the instant they were alone again.

"I have a confession to make," he said, leaning in closer, as if they weren't the only ones in the entire back room of the restaurant. As if he knew what she'd just been thinking, and from everything she'd observed about Sam, he probably did.

"And that would be what?" The question croaked from her dry throat.

"With all the Tabitha chaos, I forgot to grab the property listings from my bag in my hotel room."

His words conjured naughty, inexcusable images in her mind of what might happen if they ended up in his room. And judging from his darkening expression, Sam was thinking the same thing.

Feeling warm all over and desperate to splash some ice on both herself and the situation, Meagan reached for her only defense, her only hope of resisting Sam—words.

Meagan shifted in her seat. "That defeats the purpose of dinner, don't you think?"

"I guess that depends on whose perspective we're using," he said, his blue gaze holding hers.

Meagan's heart skipped a beat.

Sam continued, "In fact—"

The sentenced dissolved on his lips as the waiter set their plate of egg rolls in the center of the table. Sam exchanged a few comments with the man, seemingly in no hurry to finish what he'd been saying to her. Meagan, whose heart was darn near exploding with anticipation, waited anxiously for the rest of whatever he might have said. Men didn't rattle her this way, or rather, no man but Sam rattled her this way, or any way for that matter.

The waiter disappeared and Sam took a bite of his egg roll. Meagan wanted to reach across the table and strangle him for being so casual. Instead, she reached for her soda and took a long sip, forcing herself to think through the haze of arousal Sam had created in her, blaming it on pure exhaustion and no rest. She had to be reading into his words, into the energy swelling between them, or he wouldn't be so nonchalant. He'd moved on from whatever she'd thought he might say, as if it hadn't been worth saying in the first place.

"Aren't you going to eat?" he asked, snapping up a second egg roll.

"You plan on leaving me anything *to* eat?" She scooted the container of hot mustard in front of her, along with a bottle of soy sauce, and mixed them on a plate.

"We can always ask for more, and since I missed lunch, we might have to."

The prickly exterior she'd erected to protect herself slid away. He'd been there last night with her, then worked all day, and without a complaint or at least one she'd heard. He had to be as tired as she was. She put the sauce between them and set an egg roll on her plate. "You can have the last one. I had lunch, and I plan to do my meal plenty of justice when it arrives."

He gave her an appreciative murmur and dipped his egg roll into the sauce. "About the properties. One of our best bets is a beachfront house that has everything we need—privacy, size, functionality—at least on paper, that is. Oh, and not only does it have a mother-in-law house, the owner has a second house a half mile up the beach that just became available. You could use that for the crew and general whatever. Both properties would put us slightly over budget, but they might be worth fighting for."

"Wow," Meagan said. "It sounds too good to be true."

"Well, there's a catch."

"Of course," she said. "There's always a catch." She motioned with her hand. "Let me have the dirt."

"The place has been vacant for months, but now that we're considering it, there's another interested party."

"Are you sure the owner or Realtor isn't trying to manipulate us?"

"I talked with the other party," he said. "He's real

and he's eager. He's even telling the owner the show will destroy the property, referring to the wildness on other reality shows."

"Surely the owner knows the show will push up his long-term property values?"

"He knows, but he isn't willing to risk losing the rental income from the other party while waiting for us. He wants a fast answer. As in tomorrow."

"Sam, that's insane. We can't possibly decide that fast."

The waiter filled their water glasses. "Look. I'm not pressuring you here. I haven't even seen the place. On the other hand, this property has miles of open beach. You get plenty of room to film, and my team will know if anyone so much as thinks about approaching. And believe me, that'll be important." He unrolled his silverware from a napkin. "This damn curse is going to be a problem. We've already had several paranormal groups contact us, not to mention the media snooping around, looking for rumors and gossip."

"'Damn curse' is right," she murmured, sliding her napkin to her lap and picking up her egg roll only to set it back down. "We better be prepared. Once the footage I'm shooting airs, we're likely to have a three-ring circus on our hands. I hate that the studio is pressing this angle."

His brows dipped. "I thought you'd be glad for the ratings boost."

"Not like this," she said. "I mean, don't get me wrong. At first, I was just relieved to find out we didn't get cancelled. As the day has gone on, though, I'm not so sure. I worry we're headed away from the premise of the show and into trouble."

"Meaning what?"

"My father's a preacher in a small Texas town—and I'm talking small town like in the movie *Footloose*."

"So you're worried that the show may become offensive?"

"Yes and no. I want to give dance credibility and I think having real talent evolve will give it longevity, while short-term thrills and chills only give a facade of success that ultimately fizzles. The curse falls into that category in my opinion. If we build ratings on the pretense of a curse, what do we follow that with? Will dancing and the personal journeys of the dancers, who we want the audience to passionately love or hate, be enough?" She shook her head. "This curse really is a nightmare I wish I could make go away."

"I can see that," he agreed.

"Aside from the staying power issue, I've seen how a small group of people can create demons where they don't exist. It makes people irrational, and irrational can be dangerous." She took a bite of her egg roll and made a sound of pleasure. "And either this is really good or I'm just really hungry."

"I wouldn't know," he said. "I'm too hungry to be objective."

"I'm leaning toward thinking it's really good food," she said. "I'm hoping the rest of the meal is, as well."

They ate in surprisingly comfortable silence for a while before he leaned back in his chair. "I'd never have figured you for a small-town girl."

"Yeah, well, I got out of that small town the minute I could."

"And then you ended up in L.A."

"Not immediately," she said. "I went to school and that led to me producing a news program in Waco, Texas. Some random lucky breaks and I ended up in Dallas at a much larger station. A connection there gave me the chance to pitch this show. And now that I'm here, I don't want to blow it."

"Then I say we need to look at this property," he said. "The right location and security might just silence this curse nonsense. We should go check it out early tomorrow."

"That's impossible. I have footage to shoot and get edited."

The waiter appeared with their food, and Sam paused until he left, before adding, "A busy schedule is all the more reason to secure the right location and move on to other things," Sam said. "And I might be pushing a bit on this but—"

"No matter how amazing the location is, I don't have time tomorrow." She shook her head. "Not unless I can be cloned."

"I have a key," he said. "We can go after we finish here if you like. Or I can go check it out and let you know if it's a waste of time, but if it's good, you have to find time tomorrow—"

"No," she said quickly. She wouldn't be able to make the time, but she also knew this couldn't be left to someone else to decide. It was too critical to the show. "Tonight. We'll go tonight."

For several crackling seconds, they stared at one

another, and reality washed over Meagan. She'd just committed to going to a secluded beach house with Sam. She immediately picked up her fork, stabbing a water chestnut.

Sam chuckled and Meagan's eyes lifted to his. "What's so funny?"

"The absolute horror on your face when it occurred to you we'd be alone somewhere private. I can have one of my staff take you. Or you can bring along one of your staff members, if you want."

The offer surprised her. Her reaction surprised her even more, though it shouldn't have. She didn't want a chaperone. "You were some sort of Special Ops guy, right?"

"For fourteen years."

And since he was in his early thirties, that meant he'd gone into the army when he was a late teen. She wondered why, she wondered…damn it. "Then I'd say you're experienced enough to protect me," she said, shoving aside curiosity, refusing to get to know Sam any more than she felt she already did. She knew too much. She liked too much. She didn't want to like Sam.

She ate her chestnut and dabbed her mouth with her napkin. He was watching her. She could feel the warmth of those blue eyes as surely as if she were looking into them. Finally, when he didn't speak, she glanced up at him, his inspection too intense to bear, his unspoken thoughts unnerving. "Why are you looking at me like that?"

He chuckled. "I'm not sure what 'like that' means, but I was just wondering who's going to protect me from you?"

# 6

HE'D BAITED HER, unable to stop himself—expecting the flash in her eyes, and the fierceness of her expression that he found so sexy. And it had worked. For the first time since they'd sat down in the restaurant, she leaned towards him, her full lips close enough that he could imagine kissing them, as she said, "Don't tick me off and you won't need protection."

"You like being ticked off at me and you know it."

"Why would I *like* being pissed off at you?"

"At some point I think you thought it kept me at a distance. But seems to me that plan has backfired. I'm here to stay, sweetheart. Now what are you going to do with me?"

"For starters," she said, without hesitation, "if you call me 'sweetheart' again, you'll be wishing for that protection."

"I'm willing to take whatever you dish out and then some. In fact, maybe you need to unload on me and get it out of your system." He lowered his voice, all jest gone, a realization taking form. "Maybe there's a lot we need to just get out of our systems. Maybe then we can move past…it." Her eyes went wide, but she didn't lean back, didn't immediately reject the idea, didn't ask what "it" was, because they both knew. "It" was desire, hot and getting hotter by the second.

Sam didn't know what this woman did to him, but while she worried about him stealing her control, she had all but shredded his. There was something about her. Actually, everything about her worked for him, from how her forehead crinkled when she was thinking, to how passionate she was about her show. Being this interested in a woman wasn't a comfortable place to be. It wasn't uncomfortable, either. Just different for him because he couldn't seem to flip the "off" switch.

Long, sizzling seconds passed and she hadn't responded to his proposition. He arched a brow at her silence. "No snappy comeback?"

"Maybe it would just complicate things," she said, clearly talking about sex. "Maybe it would make things worse."

"My thoughts exactly up until a few minutes ago. But we damn near combust every time we're together, and it's only a matter of time before we do. We both like to maintain control, so I say we deal with this on our terms, where we control how it happens." And, he added silently, *I can finally get you alone and try to tear down the walls you've built around yourself.*

"You don't know me." She didn't sound as if she quite believed those words. "You don't know what I like."

"But I want to know. And I've known you a while now. I know things you might think I hadn't paid attention to. Like how you left a small town for a big city and now you're daring to work for a monster studio who'd eat their own young for ratings. That takes courage. On top of all of that, you're sitting here with me, alone, knowing exactly where it could lead. So I'd lay my money on you enjoying danger as long as it's on your terms." He softened his voice. "After tonight, the cameras and crew will be everywhere."

"Sam, I—"

"Meagan!"

She inhaled at the same moment he stiffened. Before he could speak, they were surrounded by a group of the crew, who'd deserted the hotel bar for the nearest restaurant. Chaos followed as tables were shoved next to each other, only a few steps away from their tiny corner. One of the cameramen—a hefty thirtysomething guy from Texas, who they all called "Double Dave" for obvious reasons—pulled a chair to their table to talk to Meagan about his "concerns" for the next day's shots. He then called yet another cameraman over to their table.

Sam listened as Meagan calmed their concerns, and then did enough listening of her own to manage to get her dinner down, while Sam did the same. He was intrigued by her expressions, her mannerisms, her respect for the people who worked for her, and knew it was a sign of just how badly he had it for this woman. She wouldn't look at him though, and he had to wonder if she was calculating a way to escape his proposition. She was good at running from him despite her obvious interest, and he wondered why.

His meal completed, Sam pushed away from the

table. "I'll check out that property, and let you know how it looks."

Meagan quickly shoved her chair back. "I'm going, too," she said. "None of the rest of this matters if we don't have a house to shoot in."

"You're viewing a property tonight?" Double Dave asked.

Sam's expression seemed to be questioning her, so she gave the same right back to him?

"We are," she said in reply to Dave, though, focused on Sam, not the cameraman. "We have to take it or lose it by tomorrow." She glanced at Dave, and the rest of the group, and then announced the exciting prospect of a new house, and that she'd report on it tomorrow.

The next thing Sam knew, he and Meagan were outside. Their eyes collided the same instant the hot, muggy air slammed into them, and their budding sexual tension expanded around them, while the world shrunk to just the two of them.

"Your vehicle or mine?" he asked, willing his body to calm.

She tilted her head, studying him with such scrutiny that it was his turn to say, "What are you looking at me like that for?"

"I just thought you were the 'I'm driving' kind of guy."

"And I thought you were the 'I'm driving' kind of woman."

"I am."

He waved her forward. "Well, then. Lead the way."

She didn't move. Instead, she stared at him intensely,

then said, "You drive. My eyes hurt from editing too much film, and I don't want you backseat driving."

"So, you'll backseat drive."

"Exactly."

Sam laughed and barely resisted the unnerving urge to grab her hand and pull her along with him—telling himself that he only needed to touch her once, that this thing was sex and sex only. He motioned her forward. "If we walk around to the side of the hotel, we can go straight to the garage and avoid another crew ambush."

"Don't you need to get the property listings from your room?"

"I put the address for this one in my GPS earlier. It's about a forty-minute drive, so we better hit the road. It's almost seven now."

Meagan groaned and they fell into step together. "I have a six o'clock shoot in the morning, and I am going to be hating life when it starts."

"Then it's good I'm driving," he said. "You can nap on the way to the property and back, if you want."

She stopped.

"What?" he asked again.

"Stop being nice to me. I liked you better when you were intentionally trying to agitate me."

She meant she felt safer, but he didn't say it, not when she could back out of their private outing before they ever left. "I simply assumed you required more rest than I do."

Her hands went to her hips. "Why would I need more rest than you? Because…" She paused, eyes lighting with understanding. "Wow. You just proved that you can bait me at will, didn't you?"

He nodded. "But you can do the same to me. Don't even think about saying you don't know it because we both know you do. We both know how to punch each other's buttons."

"Yeah," she agreed. "I guess we do."

Damn, he wanted this woman. She didn't even try and play coy with him. He liked that. He liked it a hell of a lot. "Let's get out of here before we're cornered. Or worse, before Tabitha returns."

"True," she said, her face lit with a warm smile.

At his vehicle, he held the passenger door of his Ford F150 open for her, and she gave him an awkward look. "You don't have to do that for me. I can get it."

He pressed his hand to the side of the truck, the distinctly feminine scent of her reaching him. "I'm a soldier at heart. Opening a door for a lady is as natural to me as busting my chops is apparently for you."

A rich, laugh left her lips. "I don't imagine many people 'bust your chops' easily, so I'll take that as a compliment."

"They don't and I'll take your acknowledgement of that fact as a compliment."

A subtle but obvious tension lit between them. "Actually, it is a compliment." She paused. "Sam. I, well, I've given you such a hard time that I think I should tell you how much I really appreciate how you handled the problems on set tonight. Rather than doing what I would have expected—charging in and taking over—you respected my role."

"And unless there's an imminent threat to someone's safety, I always will. My hope would be that if an unfortunate situation like that arises, you'll respect my role, as well."

"Yes. Absolutely."

"That means no running into buildings that could go up in flames any second. You wait for me."

She pursed her lips. "Unless someone is in imminent danger and I can help."

He lowered his voice. "Meagan—"

She held up her hands. "Yes. Okay. I'll wait. Probably. I'll try. And I admit running into the house wasn't one of my more brilliant moves, but I was afraid the show would go up in flames with the house. Like everyone's dreams. Everyone who'd hoped this show would change their life would have lost their dream, too. I just couldn't let that happen."

Tension curled inside Sam. Somehow, every moment he'd ever shared with Meagan, every thought he'd had, every assumption he'd made, merged into this one instant. And there lay the danger of moving forward with his intention to finally sate his hunger for her tonight.

The morning-after might not deliver the complication-free, tension-easing relief they'd both hoped for, because he simply wasn't certain that one night would be enough. And he knew combining romance with work never ended well.

Several voices sounded nearby, interrupting their moment. "Come on. We have to go before it gets any later."

She jumped into the truck, and closed the door behind her. As he rushed to the driver's side, he tried to talk himself back off the ledge, tried to convince himself not to touch Meagan, to reel himself in before it was too late. Too late? Who was he kidding? He wouldn't find the "off" switch if his life depended on it.

MEAGAN LISTENED to the engine roar to life with a fleeting realization that she didn't have her phone or her purse. She'd taken off for their dinner, expecting to stay in the hotel, with nothing in hand. Normally, she'd insist on going back for both.

Instead, she found herself fixated on Sam's powerful forearms, as he maneuvered the truck out of the parking spot. Everything about Sam was strong and powerful. His hands, his face, and his eyes, when they caught her in one of those penetrating stares.

She wanted him with as much passion as she knew he was wrong for her, which was to the point of complete and utter distraction. Worse—to the point that he was now controlling her with anticipation and fantasy.

Still, it was clear to her that avoiding him wasn't the answer, for all kinds of reasons. Sleeping with him— well, he'd offered her one night, to get "it" out of their systems. She just had to be certain there were no strings. Then, maybe he was right.

Sam sparked something inside her, consumed her without even trying. His voice, his eyes, his powerful presence, all resonated with her.

Honestly, her attraction for Sam wasn't going away, nor was he. But would making love with him extinguish the flames between them or cause them to burn brighter? Meagan admitted this had been her concern all along.

So why was she still considering it?

# 7

MEAGAN STARED AHEAD as the truck exited the garage, resisting the magnetic pull of Sam next to her, of the desire to turn to him, to study him—to slide up next to him and finally, finally, just be with him. The moon dangled low in the sky, like a lamp on an invisible chain, like her unyielding need for this man.

"Rest if you want," he said. "I'll wake you up when we get close."

"Thank you," she murmured, and sank down low in the seat and closed her eyes. She needed to think, she needed to…she didn't know. For the first time in a long time, she didn't know what she needed to do. Her mind raced to the point that she wanted to sit up, wanted to do something, anything. Instead, she pretended to sleep, sensing the shift in shadows as they maneuvered the streets of L.A., her mind playing with images. Sam looking hot. Sam looking hot while he stood in the basement dripping wet.

She forced herself to remember why she needed to concentrate. Sam might misread her, might think he had more claim to power on the set, if they slept together. They'd argue. Everyone would be affected. But then she thought of Sam's eyes when he'd walked right into the chaos earlier, when his eyes had met hers, when he'd silently asked if he could intervene.

They must have been a good thirty minutes into the ride when Sam said, "I can hear you thinking, Meagan."

She didn't pretend she wasn't awake; in fact, not pretending was a relief. She turned to face Sam. "Did you hear anything that made any sense to you, because I sure didn't."

"Want to talk about it?"

"As in—to you?"

He chuckled. It was a low, sexy sound, becoming both familiar and unnervingly likable. "I would be the only person here," he reminded her.

"Yeah, but I can't talk to you. Not about…you."

He laughed louder and cut her a look. "I can assure you with one hundred percent certainty that I know more about me than anyone else on this earth."

Fine, she'd ask him questions, but not the one really on her mind, which would be, should she sleep with him? "How old were you when you went into the army?"

"I entered on my eighteenth birthday," he said, without missing a beat, as if it was exactly what he'd expected her to ask, when they both knew it absolutely was not.

"Why?"

"It's what I was born to do, what I wanted to do. What my father, my brother and my uncles, all did."

"And you weren't scared? I mean you were a kid, Sam."

"I wasn't scared but my mother was. My brother was in Iraq at the time and my father was on active duty. She, like most spouses, found a place to tuck away the fear of losing her husband to combat. But her son, or sons, rather, were another story. She struggled to deal with the potential loss of her boys."

"I can't imagine how hard that must have been for her."

"My father saw her distress and tried to talk me into waiting a few years to enter the army," he said. "He figured that would give my mother time to get used to my brother serving. I didn't think that was the answer. I thought my mother needed to go ahead and get past her fear because the army was going to be my future. Eventually, she and I talked about it, and she gave me her blessing."

"So you went ahead and enlisted."

He nodded. "And then ended up in a fluffy desk job I didn't want. I'm pretty sure my father pulled a lot of rank to make it happen, too, though he never admitted it. Able-bodied young men do not end up at desk jobs in the army."

"I'm surprised," she said. "With him serving himself, I'd have thought he would have supported you."

"He was trying to protect my mother and he really wanted me to finish college to be eligible for officer training, which my brother rejected."

"From what I know of you, a desk job must have been hard for you to deal with."

"Oh yeah. It drove me crazy. I felt guilty for sitting at a desk while my own father and brother, and plenty of others with them, were fighting to protect our country. I would have gotten out of that desk job if I could have and I tried. It worked out though in the end. By twenty-one I'd completed my degree and I entered the officers' program, then Special Forces."

"Why Special Forces?"

"I was in for life," he said. "I wanted to be challenged and contribute everything I could, on every level possible."

Meagan absorbed those words thoughtfully, captured by him in ways she didn't want to be, didn't expect to be when she'd first met him. He was just so much more than she'd expected he'd be. This man had seen war, he'd fought to survive, and fought for the lives of others. "But you weren't in for life," she finally commented, hoping he'd explain why, nervous she might be in choppy waters he didn't want to enter.

"No," he said a bit too softly. "I wasn't in for life." He inhaled and let it out. "A few bullets in my leg took care of that."

"Oh, God, Sam," she said and added, "I'm sorry." She wanted to pull back these last words, knowing from her own injury how much she didn't like hearing them.

"Yeah, me too, because even if I could have gotten a doctor's release, which was doubtful, I knew I wasn't one hundred percent. And I wasn't willing to risk other people's lives by ignoring the reality of what I had to face."

Suddenly, her lost dream, her knee injury, felt tiny, inconsequential. "That was brave, Sam. It was very brave."

He glanced at her, surprise etched on his handsome face. "No. Those men and women out there on the front lines are the brave ones. I refused to let my ego put them at risk."

"Yes," she conceded. "They are." And he'd been one of them, he still wanted to be one of them, and couldn't. She knew how that felt, as well. How it hurt to want things you could no longer have. "Where are your parents? Are they here? Is that how you ended up in L.A.?"

"No," he said. "This is technically my home, but as a military brat, I traveled all over the place. My parents spent a good number of the last ten years in Germany, but managed to end up back in Japan just in time for the recent tsunami. Both me and my brother got a good dose of the kind of worry my mother has for her sons and her husband. We couldn't reach my parents for days. Jake—that's my brother—was on a mission overseas, and he was in rare completely freaked-out mode."

"But they're okay, right?"

He gave a quick nod of his head. "Yes. They're fine. My mother's a nurse. She was working at a Red Cross shelter at the time and refused to leave when the military families were evacuated. My father's still on active duty, and as a high-ranking officer, he had his hands full."

"I think I mentioned that my father's a preacher in a small Texas town and my mother helps with the church's volunteer efforts. We aren't really close, but I am their only child and they love me, just like I love them." She cringed at her confession, one she normally wouldn't have given, not sure why she had, and quickly moved on, "I would have gone crazy, too, not knowing if they were all right during the tsunami, or hurricane or whatever."

He glanced at her. His gaze too knowing, too aware of what she'd shared. She expected him to push her for more detail, but surprisingly, he seemed to sense she was uncomfortable, and let it pass, saying only, "Maybe you'll tell me more about them one day."

His sensitivity really floored her. "Maybe I will," she said, surprised at how much she meant it. "Tell me more about Japan and your parents."

"There's not a lot more to tell," he said. "They're fine and involved in clean-up efforts that will take years and years to complete. I went to see them right after I left the army and spent a few months helping."

There were tiny telling cracks in his voice at several places during his story. Sam wasn't at all what she'd assumed. "How'd you get hired at the studio?"

"My uncle, a retired SEAL, works for the studio. He hounded me for months to take the security job. I didn't want it. I wanted back in the army." He rubbed his right leg a bit too deeply, and she wondered just how bad his injury was, both physically and emotionally.

She opened her mouth to tell him how much she understood, and quickly snapped it shut. She didn't talk about the past. She focused on the future, like what he seemed to be doing. And my gosh, how shallow would she sound anyway? He was talking about war and sacrifice and she was upset she wasn't able to perform anymore.

"We're here," he announced, turning into a long driveway, but trees blocked her view of the house.

The ride was over and she didn't want it to be. She had enjoyed learning about Sam, which defied the idea of sex being a path to getting him out of her system.

Suddenly, she felt confused. She knew Sam was a distraction she didn't need, knew he was the kind of man that took you by storm and took over your life. Yet, on some level he was exactly what she needed. And that absolutely terrified her. She couldn't lose herself again. She couldn't. Been there, done that, didn't like it.

As soon as the truck stopped in the driveway of the two-story, towering mansion of a house, she lunged for the door handle, intending to get out as quickly as possible. She needed some distance from Sam to process her feelings.

Sam gently shackled her arm, the touch of his hand searing her skin, melting her resolve to escape him. "Hey," he said softly. "What just happened?"

He read her too easily, which only rattled her more. "Nothing. Nothing, I just—"

"Got spooked."

She hesitated, and then nodded. "Yes. I did." Somehow, her ability to be honest about her feelings made him more appealing. "I got spooked." And by the time the words were out, he was closer, still holding her arm. Still the powerful, controlling, sexy Sam, who she couldn't seem to resist.

She could smell the spicy maleness of him, warm and taunting, calling her, warming her, burning her inside out. Thank goodness for the shadowy darkness broken only by moonlight splintering through the tree limbs above them, casting their faces in shadows, hiding the damning desire surely in her eyes.

She inhaled, trying to think straight, before she did something like kiss him, instead of getting out of the vehicle. Instead, she filled her nostrils with more of that sultry male scent that made her want to stay right where she was. "Sam, I don't know what—"

"Me, either," he said, and kissed her, oh God, he kissed her, and it was wonderful. She didn't even remember him moving or how he'd become close enough to have his thigh pressed to hers. All that she knew was that his fingers were laced through her hair, his lips pressed to hers, warm and remarkably gentle—a teasing touch, following by a sweeping wash of his tongue against hers.

"Meg—"

"Don't talk," she said, her fingers curled around his neck to pull him back to her, desperate to keep this just sex, knowing deep down it might be too late. "Kiss me again."

And he did. He kissed her. No talking. No demanding things go his way, like she'd expected from him. His mouth slanted over hers, his tongue pressing past her teeth, stroking seductively against her tongue.

She moaned and arched into him, seeking more of the warmth and hardness that was so very Sam, so very right. Yet she'd have sworn he was wrong. And he was wrong for her. He was, in fact. He would be trouble but he didn't feel like trouble. Not now. Not in this moment. Okay, maybe in this very moment, she did, because she needed him. Her hands traced the rippling muscle of his shoulders.

A low growl escaped his lips, and he pulled her closer, one hand sliding up her back, molding her against his chest. His hand caressed her thigh, under her skirt. His tongue delved deeply, caressing hers in another long, lavish tasting that had her feeling it in all the places he wasn't touching, but she wanted him to be.

"You smell good," he murmured, kissing her jaw, and along to her neck. "Like vanilla and flowers. It's driving me crazy. I know we need to go see that house, and this is not the place for *this,* but I'm struggling to let you go."

The words, the gruff aroused tone of his voice, overtook her. She didn't want to let him go, either. She didn't want to think about why they shouldn't do *this.* "Then don't," she whispered, and barely had the words out before they were kissing again. A blur of passion followed, his hands all over her. Hers all over him. She was on her back, her blouse open, with him on top of her, and she barely remembered how it had happened.

Sam's phone started to ring and he tore away from her. He cursed softly, echoing the frustration she felt at the interruption. "I have to answer that."

"I know," she said, her voice breathless even to her own ears. "Especially since I don't have my phone."

"Right," he agreed, but he didn't move. "I need to get it."

She didn't want him to move. She wasn't ready to let go of this time they were sharing.

The phone stopped ringing, still he didn't move. He brushed his lips over hers. "I didn't mean for this to get so out of control. One minute we were—"

"And the next," she finished.

He smiled and pulled back to look at her, and the mood shifted, the air thickened. They stared at one another, and Meagan felt their connection in every part of herself. There was something happening between them, something that she'd never felt before, and didn't understand.

The phone started to ring again and he sighed with the inevitable demand to get up, and then, he did the most unexpected thing. Sam kissed her nose before bringing her with him to sit up.

He reached for his phone on the dash and checked the missed numbers. "It was Josh both times," Sam said. "He left a voice mail."

Meagan nodded, but she was still thinking about Sam kissing her nose. It was silly, but there was something about that small act that had her stomach fluttering.

Light flickered behind them, snapping her out of her reverie. Meagan shifted around to see a car pulling into the driveway. "Someone's here."

Sam set his phone down. "Per Josh's voice mail, Kiki insisted that he drive her out here so—"

Meagan didn't hear the rest. She shoved open the door, desperate to escape their close proximity before Kiki arrived. She tripped, and went tumbling out of the truck.

Sam was there in an instant, but she was already getting up. "Are you okay?"

"No, I am not okay! I'm embarrassed, Sam. I don't want them to know what just happened. I don't want them to think badly of either of us."

"They won't know." His gaze slid top to bottom. "Not if you button your shirt."

Her jaw dropped at the realization. Meagan rushed to fix her gaping shirt, but her fingers were shaking. "I don't do things like this. I know better. I know they backfire. Sam—"

"Easy, sweetheart," he said, wrapping her in his arms. "Take a deep breath and we'll get through this. What happens between us, is between us. No one will know."

Sweetheart. Why did that endearment sound good now, when it had bothered her before? And why did his vow that everything was going to be okay, calm her? For the first time in years, she'd felt she had her life in the palm of her hand. Neither her parents, nor her ex-boyfriends, who'd tried to control everything from her career to her politics, had control. She had control. Only tonight, she'd let this thing, whatever "it" was, with Sam, take it away from her.

"Stop calling me sweetheart, Sam."

He held her tighter and kissed her. "Whatever you say. *Meg.*"

And despite being a nervous wreck over Kiki and Josh's arrival, the familiar banter with Sam made her laugh, and that laugh had a remarkable impact. Meagan felt just a bit more in control.

She was clearly very confused.

# 8

"WHY AREN'T YOU ANSWERING your phone?" Kiki demanded the minute she stepped from Josh's black SUV. "We've been trying to reach you for over an hour. When you didn't answer, I decided to come on out here. Besides, I didn't want to miss out on the chance to be in on this very important decision."

There was accusation in everything Kiki said to Meagan, and she didn't understand it. She'd tried to break through it, to bond with the other woman over the show and it just didn't seem to be happening.

"She dropped her phone in the hotel parking lot," Sam explained before Meagan could answer. "Someone ran over it before we could get to it. The driver came damn close to running over Meagan, too."

"My God," Kiki said, her tone dripping disdain. "How in the world did you manage that?"

Sam glanced at Josh. "I left you a message to be sure everyone knew to call me if they needed Meagan."

"Sorry, boss," Josh said. The honest guilt on his face meant that either he really hadn't checked his messages, or he was a darn good actor. He inclined his head at Meagan. "My apologies for not listening to my voice mail."

"I'm sure you both had your hands full," Meagan said, repeating her earlier comment, immensely appreciative to both Sam and Josh for covering for her, but angry at herself for needing to be covered. Then to both Josh and Kiki, she asked, "Why aren't you two at the hospital?"

"I left one of the production assistants to supervise Tabitha's medical treatment," Kiki replied.

"Which P.A.?"

"I don't know." Kiki sounded snippy and impositioned. "Debbie, I think."

"Darla?" Meagan asked, hopeful.

"Yes. Darla." Kiki waved a hand. "But it doesn't matter now. I just hung up with *Darla*. She called me because she couldn't reach you. Tabitha is fine. All is well in tooth-fairy land."

Over and over Meagan had asked Kiki to start remembering everyone's names. She treated the cast horribly and tension jumped every time she was around. If Kiki wasn't related to one of the executives that had approved her show, she'd already have talked to Sabrina about firing her.

"What exactly does that mean?" Sam asked.

She shrugged. "You'd have to ask the P.A. What's going on here?"

"I called Darla myself," Josh said. "After the hospital checked her out, a dentist fitted Tabitha for some sort of temporary tooth held in with a mouthpiece, and she's now in her room resting." He glanced at Meagan. "Sam likes answers. I try to have them."

"Thank you," Meagan said, but she felt that announcement like a blow. She couldn't get answers, but Sam could?

"Why don't we head down to the property?" Sam suggested. "Then everyone can get some rest back at the hotel."

"Yes," agreed Meagan, her gaze touching his. "That sounds like a good idea."

Sam motioned her forward, falling into step beside her, while Josh and Kiki followed them. Sam glanced behind them, apparently making sure they had some distance away from the others, before softly saying, "You'll have to tell me who you ticked off to get saddled with Kiki."

It helped to hear she wasn't being overly sensitive about Kiki, and that Sam read Kiki the same way she did. "I didn't make anyone mad, except for you, that I know of. I'm pretty good at that." If there was a God of dance, she'd have said that was who she'd angered. In that case though, she would have thought her knee would have been the ultimate sacrifice, but apparently not.

"I think it's the other way around," he commented. "I'm good at making *you* mad."

"You are a master of that craft."

He laughed and darn it, she felt the sultry male baritone of it in every nerve ending of her body. There was so much about the man that appealed to her, and so many reasons not to act on what she felt for him. Yet he'd been there for her tonight in so many ways.

They cleared the trees, bringing a large shadowy property into view and Meagan paused, drinking in the cool, clean ocean air as it washed over her, calming her, if only slightly. "I already love it here. I love the ocean."

"I sure hope there are lights," Kiki said, stopping next to Meagan.

"There are," Sam answered, motioning Meagan onward, and she had the distinct impression that no matter how attractive Kiki might be, Sam wasn't impressed. The idea pleased her a little more than it should have. Another reaction she wasn't going to try to analyze at present.

Sam ran down the basics of the property as they walked. "The house is 5,000 square feet with a 2,000-square-foot mother-in-law house in the back of the main property."

"That does sound perfect," Meagan replied.

Motion detectors flickered to life, illuminating an impressive contemporary stucco house, with a balcony that wrapped around most of the second floor.

"The water is so close," Kiki exclaimed, rushing forward and calling over her shoulder. "It's amazing."

Sam sighed as Kiki expanded the distance between her and them. "I better catch up with her before she gets hurt and calls it the curse." He headed after her.

Josh fell into step with Meagan. "Kiki seems to like this place so far. Surely that's all you need to know." He grinned to let her know he was teasing her.

Meagan snorted. "That's about as true as me dropping my cell phone. I used horrible judgment by not going back to my room for my phone. It's just that if I'd gone back, I knew I'd get cornered by someone wanting to talk, and it would be even later by the time we made it out here. Still, I should have known better. Thank you for being loyal to your boss and covering for me."

"I spent the entire drive listening to Kiki talk trash about you." They started up the porch stairs, where Sam waited, having already let Kiki inside the house. "She gloated on the drive over here about how she'd saved the studio millions, insisting you'd be a failure. The worst is that she had to have known I might tell you. It's like she wanted you on edge by announcing her intent. I hate saying this because it feeds into her strategy, but Meagan, she's a cobra. Watch for the next strike, because it's coming."

Meagan crossed her arms in front of her chest, tension curling in her stomach. She had confirmation of what she'd hoped wasn't true. Not only was Kiki a true enemy, she wasn't even trying to hide her agenda.

They joined Sam at the door.

Josh glanced at Sam. "Don't worry, boss. I'll go in first, and strategically engage the enemy."

"Good luck with that one," Sam said dryly, stepping aside to let Josh enter, and then moving again to block the entrance. The porch light played on his chiseled features and full, sensual mouth—the mouth she shouldn't be looking at, but couldn't seem to resist.

"Everything okay?" he asked, towering above her, and she was struck again by the way he used his broad shoulders to shield her, this time from Kiki's potentially, most likely, prying eyes. Protective. That was the word that came to mind, rather than dominant and bossy.

"Everything is just peachy," she assured him. "In fact, tonight is just one big bucket of peachy."

Kiki peeked around Sam. "Are you coming in or what?" She disappeared.

"See," Meagan said. "Peachy."

He didn't move, his eyes narrowing a barely perceivable amount. "What's wrong?"

She lowered her voice. "You were right about watching my back with Kiki. Josh said that she bragged about saving the studio millions by getting rid of people like me. It sounds like she doesn't want the show to succeed. But—"

"Now isn't the time to talk about this, but I have your back, Meagan, and I mean that. You do what feels right and you make this as good a show as you can make it. Don't let her get to you."

Her chest tightened at the unexpectedly supportive, and yes, protective words. Right then, she realized that Sam had snuck through her defenses, into her life, and for the first time in a very long time, if only for tonight, it was a relief to not feel alone. She nodded. "I know. You're right."

"I don't think you do." There was nothing accusing in his tone, no taunt, none of their normal word play.

"I do. I know." Her lips lifted ever so slightly. "But it helps to be reminded. Thank you."

He studied her and then gave a small incline of his head, flattening himself against the door to let her pass.

As Meagan moved by Sam, her shoulder brushed his chest. She froze with the impact, her gaze momentarily meeting his, heat glimmering in the depths of his stare. And she didn't look away, or hide from him, or herself. She wanted Sam. She was so very tired of denying herself this man.

But their window to be alone was now gone. Meagan had no doubt that Kiki would notice if they disappeared after this and didn't show up back at the hotel, which was all but a film set, with cameras and people everywhere.

Kiki might not be able to steal her show, but she'd definitely stolen her one night with Sam. While it was probably for Meagan's own good, it didn't feel that way right now. Meagan believed she would regret this lost chance for a very long time.

# 9

SAM TRAILED MEAGAN INTO the house, more than a little concerned about Kiki. He saw her actions, her using Josh to taunt Meagan, as confirmation that she felt invincible. Sabrina was right, Kiki was dangerous.

In the kitchen, Sam's gaze drifted over Meagan's skirt and the way it hugged her cute, tight backside. He liked that backside, but more so, he *liked* Meagan. This woman was under his skin and going nowhere but deeper fast. When he'd watched her fight through her worries over Kiki, when he'd seen the determination to succeed reignite in her eyes, he'd been blown away. Meagan was sexy, feisty, and passionate about what she believed in. And that made him passionate about her. He wasn't going to let anyone, especially Kiki, tear her down.

"The setup is perfect," Meagan said, descending a few steps to a sunken living room, and turning to face him. She pointed toward the open kitchen, where Kiki leaned on the island counter, and Josh stood stoically next to her.

"The way the kitchen overlooks the main area is terrific for panned shots," Kiki agreed, actually sounding as if she really cared about the show.

"I love it," Meagan said, holding out her arms, as if embracing the room. "I can only pray the upstairs is as terrific as the downstairs."

That's when Sam did a silent "Oh, crap." The buttons of Meagan's blouse were uneven, obviously hurriedly secured. If that blouse didn't scream an announcement about what he and Meagan had been doing in his truck when Josh and Kiki arrived, he didn't think anything would.

Cautious to appear casual, Sam sauntered toward Meagan. He stood so that his big body blocked the others' view of the problem he knew would panic Meagan if she discovered it.

"It's a unique setup," he explained, two fingers pointing to the left of the living room, by the kitchen. "These stairs lead to a section of the top floor." He then indicated the opposite side of the room, where he intended to herd Meagan and quickly. "Stairs on that side lead to a completely separate second level. Since sleeping arrangements are so important, why don't we have a look up there now?"

Meagan's eyes went wide, and she brushed her windblown hair from her face. "I searched everywhere for split quarters when the show was starting, and I couldn't find anything. I had to convert a downstairs den to a bedroom in the other house."

"So I was told by the studio," he said. "But I can't take credit. Josh did the legwork." He gestured toward the stairs. The ones nowhere near Kiki. "Shall we head up?"

Meagan frowned, studying him a moment. "Okay." She began climbing the stairs, but the instant they were behind the wall encasing the steps, she turned to him and whispered, "Now it's my turn to ask. What's wrong?"

Sam was shocked that she'd read his discomfort. He was special ops, trained to be unreadable. And he was cautious enough to know better than to risk her freaking out about her blouse if he told her. "Just concerned about the property," he assured her. "If the bedroom situation won't work, even if I approve the security profile, the house is worthless, don't you think?"

Her brows furrowed, and she looked as if she might question him again. Instead though, she gave a little nod. "Yes. You're right, of course." She headed up the stairs.

For a second Sam just stared after her, wondering what this woman was doing to him, and why he was powerless to stop it. Not that he wanted to, but he wasn't on sure footing which was unsettling. Fortunately, before leaving the main room he'd discreetly motioned to Josh to keep Kiki occupied, before he'd headed upstairs after Meagan.

MEAGAN WALKED THROUGH the spacious upstairs bedrooms, her mind on Sam, who'd officially done exactly what men like Sam—strong, dominant types—did to those around them. He had taken control. But even as the thought occurred, as she knew that she was somehow villainizing him, she admitted he didn't deserve that from her. And that made Meagan want to scream, and not at Sam, but at herself. He wasn't trying to be controlling, and in fact, he'd surprised her with how sensitive he was to her own need for control of the show. If he had control, it was because she'd given it to him. She was powerfully affected by everything the man did—or didn't do, for that matter.

There was a part of her that reveled in being so blown away by Sam, and another that was reeling from him knocking her off guard. She wanted to keep her distance, but again, the logic, while smart, didn't appeal in the slightest.

Meagan passed a bathroom and entered the large master suite, which could accommodate three contestants, but would only need to host two. And what a master it was. Huge double windows led onto what appeared to be a balcony. She needed to get Kiki up here and assign her furniture-shopping duty. With cameras rolling, that wasn't an unimportant task.

"Meagan?" Sam's voice and the sound of big feet climbing the stairs echoed nearby.

"In the master," she called, and headed into the bathroom. Wow. If she were selfish, she'd find a way to make this her suite and her bathroom. There was a separate shower in a sort of rock enclave that was envy worthy, and a deep sunken tub equally so, as well as a double vanity and a huge closet. The girls would have to draw straws for the room. It would be the only fair way to manage them choosing.

Footsteps closed in on her, and her stomach fluttered with the awareness of Sam being nearby. Her stomach had actually fluttered. When in the world had that last happened with a man?

She didn't turn, afraid she'd give away what she

was feeling, but she knew the instant Sam entered the bathroom.

Meagan gasped at the daring, impossibly damning action of him shutting the door, and right then she was sure she had been wrong. Sam was bad news; Sam was still the chaos she thought he was.

She reeled at the sight of her hot soldier, all big and tall. "What are you doing? What are you thinking?"

"I'm thinking your shirt is buttoned crooked, and you need to fix it now, before Kiki notices it."

Her jaw dropped, and then her mouth formed a silent "Oh," before she quickly started to right the buttons. "Oh, God. Oh, God. Did they see? Did Kiki see?"

"No," he said. "Why do you think I all but shoved you toward the stairs and then sent them to inspect other parts of the house? But they will be here any minute."

She checked her blouse in the mirror. "Thank you, Sam. Thank you so very much." This time the appreciation came freely and without an ounce of hesitation. Time and Kiki were all that mattered. Task completed, she patted down the wild mess of her dark hair and turned to him, holding out her hands to her sides. "Please tell me I have covered all evidence of our earlier…that nothing else is where it shouldn't be."

"You're perfect," he said softly, his eyes hot, his voice warm. He yanked open the bathroom door, eliminating any chance they would be caught in a compromising position. Or so she thought. Before she knew his intentions, Sam pulled her into the enclave of the shower, melding her body to his.

"I hate that we were interrupted," he confessed, an instant before his mouth closed down over hers. The assault on her senses was instant—a tangled ball of fear of being caught, and intense, nerve-prickling awareness. His tongue touched hers, suckling and licking, until she moaned and melted into his kiss, his body—correction—his hard masculine body.

Meagan grappled for willpower, her hands going to his shoulders, as she tried to convince herself to push away from him. He just tasted too good, and felt so wonderful.

"We shouldn't be doing this," she whispered, forcing her mouth from his.

His voice lowered, became husky. "And aren't you glad we are?"

"Yes," she whispered, her hands sliding around his neck, her breasts melding to his chest, her lips meeting his again. Meagan felt herself drift away, unable to stop it from happening. This man stole her reason, her presence of mind. There was no show, no Kiki, just her and Sam. Until there were footsteps and voices and a dart of adrenaline shot through her bloodstream.

She tried to pull away. Sam held her, and pressed his lips to her ear. "I can't wait to finally have you to myself." His teeth scraped her lobe before he set her away from him. She didn't know how he planned to have her to himself, but if her trembling with need was any indication, she hoped he had a way.

"Hello! Hello!"

It was Kiki, and Meagan shook herself, quickly checking the mirror, about to rush from the bathroom, when Sam yelled, "In here, Kiki."

Meagan turned to him and mouthed, "Are you crazy?"

He arched a brow, as if he had no idea why she would ask such a thing.

Kiki appeared in the doorway, a frown on her pretty face. "What's going on?"

Sam indicated the sink. "Ants. If you two want this place, I'll need to get an exterminator written into the agreement prior to move-in."

"Oh good grief," Kiki exclaimed. "There's a ton of them."

And sure enough, there were a ton of them. Meagan barely bit back a smile. Sam was a phenomenal kisser, and really brilliant to boot.

"You have to see the mother-in-law house," Kiki said. "It has three rooms, so I can stay with you and not have to drive out every day."

Okay, so there went her lusty, Sam-created high. "Let's go check," Meagan said.

She moved forward, toward Sam, and his eyes twinkled with mischief and the promise of more kisses, more touches, more fire. Promises she really wanted him to keep. Besides. She owed him a thank-you for telling her about her buttons.

Meagan exited the bathroom with him on her heels, their shared secrets somehow uniting them beyond the passion they shared. And for the first time in a long time, she admitted to herself that having someone at her back wasn't such a bad thing, not when that someone was Sam, at least so it seemed.

The realization puzzled her. Oh sure, she'd been standing alone for a long while—beating a path through the entertainment industry with a family that didn't approve and hardly spoke to her. And sure, she'd tried a few times to escape into a man's arms, into a relationship with a Beta-type guy, when deep down she knew alphas appealed far more. But she also knew that alphas were demanding and controlling, and she'd seen enough of that in her small town to last a lifetime—they'd sent her running for the hills. Sam was alpha—one hundred percent all-hot alpha male. So why wasn't she running from him?

# *10*

ONLY FIFTEEN MINUTES after the bathroom kiss, they'd looked at the mother-in-law house and were on to the additional house a mile away that was also part of the lease. Meagan was in the backseat of Josh's SUV, all too aware of her leg intimately pressed to Sam's. Kiki was in the front. Kiki, who Meagan couldn't escape, any more than she could the memories of being in Sam's truck, and what they'd done together. It all threatened to suffocate her right here and now.

"I can't get over how perfect the mother-in-law house was," Kiki said, glancing around the seats at Meagan. "We'll be roommates."

"Perfect." Except for the fact that there had been only two bedrooms, one of which Kiki had excitedly claimed. "We haven't seen the second property yet."

"That'll be for security," Kiki said, glancing at Sam. "Surely you can work with whatever you get, right?"

And bless Sam, he simply said, "We'll see," once again, leaving the power in her hands, doing exactly the opposite of what she'd wrongly assumed he would do.

She wanted to crawl into his lap and kiss him. Though she was pretty sure, he could tick her off right now, and she'd still want him just as much.

MEAGAN SOON STOOD ON the back deck of the extra house, hands on a balcony railing overlooking the dark beach. Unseen waves were crashing on the shoreline and Sam was by her side. Kiki, thankfully, was off somewhere on her cell phone.

"It works for you?" she asked him.

"I'd say the setup is about as perfect as you can get on such short notice, with such a small timeframe to move in and start filming."

A soft purr—or more like a meow—sounded close by. "Did I just hear a cat?" Another meow, muffled but nearby. She pushed off the railing, trying to figure out where it was coming from, and Sam did the same. "Could it be trapped, Sam? Here kitty, kitty. Here kitty." More meowing.

Sam walked down the steps that led to the beach, making a motion with his hands for her to keep calling the cat. Meagan followed him, and the sound. "Here kitty, kitty. Here kitty."

Sam kneeled down at the bottom step, and the next thing she knew, he was holding a kitten.

Meagan rushed forward. A cute little ball of white fur in Sam's hands. "Is it okay?"

"Let's go up to the porch where the light is better and check it out."

Meagan rushed up the stairs. Sam's big hand was like a hammock cradling the kitten. "Oh, how sweet," she said, as it curled on top of Sam's palm. "Oh, no." She shifted the animal a bit. "There's a cut, Sam. It looks bad. It's deep."

"Yeah," he agreed. "She needs a vet as soon as possible before infection sets in."

Meagan glanced at him, surprised. "You'd be okay with that? With us taking it to the vet on the way back to the hotel?"

"Oh, my God!" Kiki said. "Is that a rat?"

"It's not a rat." Meagan grimaced. "A kitten, Kiki."

"Well, keep it away from me," she said. "I'm allergic."

The look on Sam's face said he'd had all of Kiki he could take for one night. "We should be leaving anyway," he said. "We all have an early morning, and we need to take the cat by a vet." The kitten meowed loudly, as if in agreement.

"That thing can't ride with us," Kiki said. "Seriously. I'm allergic."

A muscle in Sam's jaw tensed, and he spoke directly to Meagan. "How do you feel about walking back to the truck? It's not quite a mile down the beach. The owner has beach lights we can turn on here and turn off at the other house."

"I don't mind walking at all."

They wrapped the kitten in a jacket that Josh had stashed in his SUV and started toward the first house, the breeze off the ocean chilling the air. "I feel like I keep saying this tonight, but thank you for this, Sam."

"You don't have to thank me. I would have taken the kitten to the vet, with or without you."

Her chest tightened with yet another unfamiliar emotion. "You keep surprising me, Sam."

He stopped abruptly, and faced her. "What…you thought I was mean to children, elderly people and animals?"

"No!" she quickly said. "No, it's just that—"

He started walking again. She trailed after him. "Sam."

"We need to get to the vet," he said. "And we both know that you made a ton of assumptions about me." He cut her a sideways glance. "Bet you didn't realize that Special Forces are also focused on humanitarian missions, did you? That we spend a huge portion of our careers helping people, and yes, animals, who can't help themselves."

Guilt slid into her gut. "No. I thought soldiers were soldiers. They fought wars."

"Unfortunately, we often have to fight to give the aid to those who need it. But there is nothing like seeing hope in the face of someone who—regardless of age, race, sex, religion or nationality—thought the world had forgotten them. It's something worth getting up for every day."

An injury had stolen that from him. More guilt filled her. "I guess there's a lot I didn't know."

"And a lot you assumed."

"Yes."

He glanced her way. "And?"

"And what?"

"And you know exactly what."

"Fine. I'm sorry. But don't tell me you didn't make assumptions about me."

"You're right," he agreed. "I did."

"And?" she prodded right back, seeking her apology. They stopped a few feet from the truck.

"And I'm not apologizing because so far I've been right about every assumption I've made. You're stubborn, controlling—"

"I am not controlling!"

"Determined, hardworking and a great kisser." He handed her the bundle in his arms. "Hold on to her so I can turn off the beach lights and unlock the truck."

"Her?"

"Yeah. Her."

A female. She liked that. "Then I think I'll call her *Sam*antha, because she's so sweet and cuddly—*just like you*." She snorted. He arched a brow, but didn't comment.

Instead he clicked the lock on the truck and opened the door. Meagan slid inside, careful with the meowing kitten that she stroked and talked to.

Then, to her surprise, Sam leaned into the truck and laid a sexy, hot kiss on her, his tongue delving past her lips for a slow, sensual exploration before he said, "We both know that not only am I not sweet and cuddly, you like that about me." And then he was gone, shutting the door behind him.

He was right—he wasn't sweet and cuddly. He was a big, sexy alpha lion, and she couldn't wait to see if she could make him purr for her. And there it was. For the first time in a long, long time, a man was a challenge. It excited her. He excited her.

IT WAS AFTER MIDNIGHT when Sam stepped off the elevator with Meagan by his side, and headed along the hotel floor, toward her room. Samantha's cut hadn't been nearly as bad as they'd thought, and she'd received a thumbs-up and a follow-up appointment from the vet.

Sam carried several overstuffed bags filled with an assortment of feline supplies, including a pink bed to match the pink bag in which Meagan was carrying Samantha. Long before the trip to the 24-hour Walmart, where she'd purchased half the pet-supplies department and declared Samantha the show's new "good luck charm," he'd known that she was going to be heartbroken if an owner showed up to claim the tiny fur ball. While at the vet, they'd had time to talk, and they'd decided they'd fight for the property, and Sam had promised to investigate where the kitten might have come from.

They stopped at her room door and their eyes met, instant electricity crackling between them, as it had so many times tonight—and well before tonight, too.

Samantha made a soft meow, and Meagan jerked her gaze from Sam's, swiping at the door with the plastic key she'd pulled from her pocket. She held the door open and went inside. He didn't. Several eternal seconds passed before Meagan grabbed his arm and tugged him forward.

"Sam, damn it, hurry up, before someone sees you." She shut the door behind him and locked it—assuming he would stay.

"I wasn't aware I was invited in."

She ignored the comment and sat down on the floor to let a meowing Samantha out of her bag. Sam laughed as the animal rubbed against her leg and purred up a storm.

Meagan and Sam squatted by the pink bed, where Samantha proceeded to plop down next to the catnip-enhanced stuffed animal that Meagan had bought for her, and go to sleep.

Both Sam and Meagan laughed. "She's so cute, Sam. I hope we don't find an owner. I want to keep her."

Their eyes locked and the air around them seemed to thicken and capture them.

"I know you do," he said softly. She'd told him about the pets she'd had growing up. There was something about Meagan. Something about the vulnerability beneath the guard she erected to protect herself, that spoke to him well beyond the desire he had for her. It made him prod her for pieces of her life, to understand her.

"I worked so many crazy hours in the newsroom that I didn't feel I could have a pet," Meagan said, stroking the kitten's back.

"How does dance and the newsroom fit together?" he asked. "I haven't quite figured out the connection."

Her lashes lowered and he could feel the sudden tension in her. "One of my teachers in high school once worked at Julliard before she had a car accident and a back injury she never fully recovered from. Her family owned some property in our community so she took a job teaching English, which was her second major. Anyway, she found out how intrigued I was by ballerinas and she secretly started teaching me to dance."

"Secretly?" he asked, sensing there was a whole lot of pain behind this story, and wanting to understand it, to understand her.

"My parents wouldn't have approved," she said. "When I told you the town I grew up in was like the town in the movie *Footloose,* I wasn't joking. When I started dancing in college my parents were sure the devil had stolen their only child's soul to test their faith. It was…difficult." She waved a hand as if to wave away the problem. "Long story short, when a television station came to a career day at my college, I hit it off with one of their recruiters, and they offered me a job. It wasn't dancing, but the production end of things really struck a chord with me. I like making things come together."

"It seems pretty darn stressful."

"It is, although that only makes it all the more rewarding when everything does come together." The kitten meowed and the shadows in Meagan's eyes disappeared. "She's just too cute. I think I'm in love."

In love. The words hit him hard. He'd never been in love. He'd never before even said the word in the same sentence as he had a woman's name. But Meagan…there was something about her. She made him feel things he'd never felt. One night. Right. That had been a joke. There was no way one night would ever be enough with this woman. These past few hours had proven that to him.

Sam watched her playing with the kitten, digesting what she'd told him, wanting to press for more. And there was more. He knew there was, but he forced himself to take things slow, not to pressure her. He got why this show meant so much to her now though. She has a passion for dance that she'd had to walk away from, and now had a chance to experience again in some way.

"I think your new cat needs a dog pal," Sam said.

"A Lab, right?" she asked. "A cat and a Lab, like you said you had on the military base."

He liked her reference to what he'd shared with her during the vet visit. "Exactly."

"Well, then," she said. "If the show gets renewed for a second season, I'll get Sam a Lab to celebrate."

"Sam? As in me or the cat?"

"I guess you could share." She looked away, as if she realized she'd inferred he'd still be around then, involved in her life. And if she didn't, he sure did.

Sam slid a finger under her chin, lifting her gaze to his. "That sounds like a deal to me."

Suddenly, they both moved into each other's arms and were kissing wildly, passionately, hands roaming, tongues teasing.

"Either tell me to leave now, Meagan," he rasped near her ear, "or tell me to stay and make love to you."

Her fingers stabbed into his short hair, shoving his head back so she could search his face. "I know I should tell you to go. I do. Every piece of me says that work and pleasure are a bad combination but—"

"Stay or go, sweetheart."

Seconds ticked by like hours before she whispered, "Stay, Sam. I want you to stay."

# 11

SAM CONFUSED HER. He seduced her. And with his big body pressed to hers, her skirt up to her hips, his hot mouth devouring hers, he consumed her. She didn't want to be consumed by Sam, but at the same time, it was *all* she wanted—and she wanted it so badly, wanted *him* so badly, the mere existence of clothing between them was like sandpaper against her skin.

"One night," Meagan panted against his lips. "We do what you said in the restaurant. We get this thing between us out of our systems." But even as she made the declaration, she doubted that possibility. There was something about this man that drew her, that reached insider her and spoke to her.

"We can try," he replied, and before she could question his answer, his mouth slanted over hers. Meagan's resistance to that kiss lasted all of a second. She'd fought this attraction to Sam for so very long, and she had no more fight in her, not where he was concerned.

His tongue caressing hers, and she could taste the hot coffee they'd drank at the vet clinic. It reminded her of how he'd been there for her, both when Kiki jabbed at her, and when she'd wanted to help the kitten.

Meagan didn't resist as Sam pulled her to her feet and picked her up. He was big and strong, and it felt good to just be with him. To just forget everything except for what was happening right now.

They went down on the bed together, him on top of her, the weight of him, the feel of him, as erotic as anything she'd ever felt. As *right* as anything she'd ever felt. Again she thought of him by her side tonight, facing challenges with her, and it had been good. Too good. It scared her. He scared her. She'd never had anyone create this kind of feeling in her. She could lose herself to this man, her identify, and just then, she didn't care.

"I've wanted you since the first time I saw you," he whispered, his lips by her ear, his hand sliding through her hair, down her shoulder, over her breast. "Do you remember when that was?"

"Yes," she said, barely finding her voice as he pressed kisses along her jaw. She could feel his arousal, thick and hard between her legs. She could feel herself shaking with desire. She couldn't believe she was here, like this, with Sam. "You tried to take the Dr. Pepper I'd paid for, that had gotten lodged in the machine."

His eyes found hers. "I paid, too. You knew that. You just wanted to fight with me."

She wrapped her arms around his neck, a smile tugging at her lips. "Maybe."

His lips brushed hers. "Why?"

"Why do you like to fight with me?"

"Call me a sadist, but it turns me on when you throw darts at me with your eyes."

She laughed and said his name, simply because it felt right on her tongue. "Sam."

The mood shifted with that one whispered word. Gone was the playful banter. Sam leaned in and kissed her, a soft, gentle kiss, a short slice of his tongue teasing hers. So light, so simple, but so intense, so completely overwhelming. And when he pulled back to look at her, to study her, his blue eyes simmered like crystals in the sunlight, desire burning deep in their depths. But there was more in his expression, so much more. There was tenderness, and it was so unexpected, it stole her breath away. His fingers teased her breast. Her skin burned wherever his fingers touched, and goose bumps chased the heat.

He reached up and pulled his shirt over his head, tossing it aside. She traced the rippling muscle of his shoulders, his arms. He was beautiful, the kind of man that was sculpted from hard work and sweat, but in his case, from honor and bravery, from serving his country.

He worked the buttons on her blouse, struggling to unhook them. She did it for him, and she didn't shy away when his gaze held hers, and that act held meaning. She wanted him to know that she was willingly undressing for him, not doing it in a moment of complete abandon like in the truck. This was a choice, and one she wasn't going to let herself regret.

They didn't speak, as if they were both afraid some magical spell would be lifted and this would end before it ever began. Once the buttons were unhooked, his lips kissed her collar bone, his fingers traced the top of her black bra, shoving down the silk to tease her nipples. Meagan moaned at the intimate exploration, her thighs aching, her body hot with need that only Sam could answer.

When finally her blouse was off and her bra, too, Sam worked her skirt down her hips, taking the slash of black panties down with it. She'd barely kicked away her shoes before he tugged her to the end of the mattress, and went down on his knees between her legs. He caressed her then, and she trembled with anticipation.

"Just so you know," he said. "I'm going to do everything to make sure one night isn't enough for you." His lips pressed to her stomach, his fingers sliding into the wet heat of her body.

No. One night wasn't enough. Right now, it felt like too much. Too much pleasure, too much desire, too much yearning. But no. Not enough of Sam.

SAM TOOK HIS TIME with Meagan, savoring every blissful second with her. How he'd ever thought sex would work Meagan out of his system, he didn't know. His lips traveled the dip of her flat stomach, the curve of her hip. His nostrils flared with the soft feminine scent of her perfumed skin. He moved lower down her body. His breath teased her clit, and she arched into him, silently asking for more. Her sex tightened around the two fingers inside her, telling him he was pleasing her. And pleasing her was exactly what he burned to do.

Sam's cock thickened, his body pulsing with the need to be inside her, reacting to how readily she responded to him. With any other woman her willingness to give herself to him wouldn't have impacted him with such force. But with Meagan, it did. It did because he knew she didn't give herself easily. It mattered because she meant something to him, because what she felt and needed and wanted mattered to him in a way it had never mattered before.

Sam lapped at the swollen nub, his fingers gently massaging the tight wet heat of her body. Her soft moans driving him crazy, pressing him onward to hear another and another. He lifted her leg over his shoulder, licked her and teased her until he felt her body clench and begin to spasm. Slowly, delicately, he suckled her, easing her through her release.

To his surprise, she covered her face with her hands, as if she were embarrassed. She was one big wonderful surprise after another, this woman. Feisty and confident one minute, and insecure and sensitive the next. Sam kissed her stomach and slid her farther onto the bed. "You're beautiful. I loved doing that to you."

"Sam," she said shyly, her lashes fluttering, her cheeks turning rosy.

He smiled as he watched her blush. "Don't go anywhere," he told her before he moved away from her to finish undressing.

She lifted up on her elbows to watch him, the timidness of moments before sliding away. Her gaze lingered on his body, her expression hot with interest. And when she scraped her teeth over her bottom lip, his cock jerked and hardened. He started for the bed, and then silently cursed his eagerness, grabbing his pants and pulling a condom from his pocket.

And though he was beyond aroused, beyond reason, he didn't miss the distressed look that flashed across her face. "I don't carry condoms with me, sweetheart. I wasn't, however, going to miss a night with you because I didn't have one. I got a few when we stopped at the store." He tossed two extras on the bed.

Her lips curved instantly and she nodded her pleasure at that answer. "Can I?" she asked, scooting to sit at the end of the bed and holding out her hand.

"You don't even have to ask," he assured her. Every muscle in his body was tense with anticipation as he stepped forward.

She took the package from him and opened it, then wrapped her soft hand around his hard cock, the contrast almost too much for him. When he thought she'd slide the condom on him, she instead slid her tongue over his erection.

Sam sucked in a breath, desire rushing through him, tightening his balls. His hand went to her shoulder. "As much as I like that, I'm about as on edge as a man can get."

"I like that you're on edge," she said softly. "I like knowing you feel what I feel."

Her words were like fuel on the fire that was his need for this woman. He took the condom from her and rolled it on, before he moved them both to the middle of the bed. He spread her legs, settling between them, fitting his shaft into the warm V of her body.

He kissed her before she could say anything more, claiming her mouth, just as he pressed inside her.

Sam buried himself to the hilt, the tight feel of her squeezing him, driving him wild. She gasped into his mouth with the impact, whispering his name. He wanted to hear her say his name like that over and over. He could never hear it enough.

He pulled back to look at her, seeking a glimpse of

the passion on her face. When his eyes met hers, he felt the punch in his gut, the connection that defied one night of sex. And when he did start to move, to make love to her, passion expanded that look, that emotion. A gripping sensual rhythm quickly built, until they were crazy with kissing each other, rocking and pumping, both trying to get closer, to get more of each other. And when they eventually collapsed together, Sam pulled her into his arms and held her. They lay like that for a long while, her head on his shoulder, her hand on his chest.

Sam turned to his side to face her, and she did the same, curling her hand under her head like a pillow. "Tell me more about the town you grew up in," he prodded, wanting to learn everything about her.

She laughed. "We're naked and you want to hear about the town I grew up in? They'd be appalled that we're laying here naked and having a conversation, I can tell you that for sure. Apart from that there's really nothing to tell."

"How do your parents feel about you scoring a national television show?"

"I don't talk to them about it," she said. "We decided years ago that it was the only way we could handle my decisions."

"You can't mean they don't approve of the show?"

Immediately, he could sense the tension in her. Sam reached over and brushed her hair out of her eyes. "I'm sorry. I didn't mean to upset you."

She wet her lips and looked at him. "I know you didn't. And every time I tell myself I don't care what they think, that their opinion of me doesn't hurt, something happens and it does again."

"They really think what you're doing is bad?"

She nodded. "Yes. They do."

Sam took her into his arms. "Well, all I see is a beautiful, successful woman, who inspires me with how she charges after her dreams. Albeit, a little bossy, but I apparently like that in a woman."

She smiled and kissed him. "Do you now?"

"Seems that way."

"Maybe I should test you," she said, and pushed him to his back, before climbing on top of him. And all Sam could say was *please* and *more*. He wanted more.

# 12

MEAGAN SHOT FROM THE DEPTHS of a hard sleep to a sitting position. Her gaze tracked around the hotel room—Sam. Where was Sam? Gone. He was gone, and for reasons she was too groggy and panicked over to fully grasp. The realization twisted her stomach into knots. And, oh God, what time was it? And where was the ringing phone?

She scrambled across the mattress that smelled of musky male sensuality and grabbed for the phone, her legs twisted in a sheet. Under said sheet she was naked. She'd been very naked, and very happy being naked, with Sam. Who, she was reminded again, was gone. And she really didn't want to know what time it was, considering the prospect of being late to set was very real at this point.

She grabbed for the receiver and it fell. She cursed and yanked the cord, bringing the receiver to her ear. "Hello?"

"Wake-up call, sweetheart."

"Sam." His voice did funny things to her knotted

stomach. "What time is it?" She reached for the clock at the same moment that he said, "Five-fifteen. You have forty-five minutes to be on set."

Samantha meowed loudly.

He chuckled. "I hear the cat. She wants to be fed as badly as I'm betting you want to go back to sleep."

"Please tell me no one saw you leave."

"No one saw me leave."

"You're—"

"Absolutely positive, which is why I left when it was still a ghost town, when I honestly wanted to stay in bed with you."

A memory of him curled around her, *spooning,* flashed in her mind. It was the last thing she remembered. She'd told herself she'd only lay there a minute and then she'd get up, she'd send him away, but she hadn't wanted to send him away. She'd wanted him to stay.

"Although," he added, "you do snore."

"I do not snore!" She scooped up the meowing kitten who was trying to climb up onto the bed, and put her on the bedspread.

"You now have forty-one minutes until set, and a hungry, loud kitten on your hands." His voice softened. "And yes. You do snore. I guess I'll have to record you next time to prove it."

Next time? Next time. He'd said next time. "Sam—"

It was too late. He'd hung up.

FOUR HOURS LATER, Meagan still hadn't seen Sam, and she hated how much she pined for when she would. But she'd managed to get enough footage of the contestants and hotel, which the curse had forced them into, to head to the editing room at the rehearsal studio. She'd told everyone to rest. They'd practice at the rehearsal studio again the next morning.

And so it was outside the editing room, after she'd sent her crew to have some dinner, that Meagan entered the tiny break area of the production facility. There, Meagan finally came face-to-face with Sam. She was struggling to get the package of peanuts she'd purchased from one of the two snack machines when it happened. She was actually *facing* the machine when the tingling awareness started—the same tingling awareness she'd felt in the executive offices, a sensation she'd been too flustered then to identify. But she felt it now, and knew what it meant.

"Sam," she said softly, steeling herself for the impact that seeing him again would have. And she'd been right to steel herself because if Sam had stolen her breath before she'd slept with him, he absolutely sucked it straight out of her lungs now.

He stood there, gloriously male, with one broad, perfect shoulder resting on the doorjamb, his jaw shadowed, already fighting the blade of his morning shave.

"Problem?" he asked, his eyes raking over her slim-fitted jeans and studio T-shirt, as if she were naked. And, heaven help her, the real problem was how many times she'd replayed being exactly that way with him today.

She nodded. "The *curse* appears to have targeted my peanuts."

His sexy, wickedly capable mouth curved upward, and he pushed off the wall. "Let me see what I can do."

He sauntered toward her, and she fought the urge to stay right there in front of the machine, right there in his path. She was losing her mind. Sam was making her lose her mind, distracting her from her job, her dream, and the career she had as the only means of supporting herself. And yet, she wanted to touch him, to feel the warmth of him again. She realized then, that on some level, she'd push Sam away. Since she now knew he wasn't just an alpha male who made her tingle when he entered the room. What he made her feel was awareness on a much deeper level. The kind of thing you were lucky to experience, and so you didn't simply shut it off. Lucky. Yes. She couldn't ignore what she felt for him. She didn't want to.

Meagan didn't move. She stood in front of the machine, and he stopped in front of her. They stared at each other, neither speaking. They didn't have to. The air around them all but combusted.

His fingers brushed her cheek. "You look tired, Meg."

"Meagan," she corrected, fighting the shiver of arousal rushing down her spine.

He smiled. "Whatever you say, sweetheart."

Voices sounded somewhere in the distance and her heart raced. The last thing she needed was her crew talking about her affair with Sam, especially with Kiki out for blood. Not that Meagan was having an affair with Sam. She didn't know what she was doing with Sam. Confusion balled up inside her. "Don't call me sweetheart, either. I said one night, Sam." She hated herself for saying that, and she wanted to take the words back. She didn't even know why she'd said them.

He continued to stare at her, his expression unreadable. "Yes," he finally said. "You did."

There was a sharp quality to the two words that cut her deeply. Just as she'd thought, she pushed him away and didn't mean to. It felt bad. Really bad. "I just…we can't…I just don't want people to see so that's why I said no touching and no sweetheart—"

"And no kissing. Got it. I'll stick to rescuing your peanuts." He didn't sound happy and his mood seemed to darken instantly.

She expected him to shake the machine. Instead, he stuck change in the slot and punched a button. Before she knew it, he'd secured two bags of peanuts, and two Dr. Peppers.

He held up one of the sodas. "I believe I owe you this." He claimed a chair and then tossed out bait to get her to sit with him. "I have news about the contestants' house. Join me and I'll tell you all about it."

"More bribery?"

He arched a brow. "Is it working?"

"Apparently very well." She sat down across from him, and truthfully she was relieved to have a few more minutes with him, to be able to fix whatever she'd broken. "What about the house?"

"They agreed to all my requests, including the exterminator. If you're sure you want the place, then I can have it ready for you to move in by the weekend. That should give you time to get settled before you have to *go live* in the house. And frankly, I'd prefer having the contestants there and contained, rather than at a hotel where I can't be sure they're really in their rooms and safe." He popped open his drink.

There was something about the way he said that statement. "What happened that I don't know about?"

"A tabloid reporter tried to sneak onto the floor dressed as a waiter."

She shook her head. "Like I don't have enough to worry about. Now this?"

"You don't have to worry about this. That's what I'm here for. And that's why I would rather get us to the new house now, rather than later."

"Yes," she said. "Please. The sooner the better. I'm all for as much control as I can get, and as quickly as possible."

Their eyes locked, thick silence stretching between them. "I aim to please, Meagan," he said, finally.

Meagan. Not Meg. Not sweetheart. That should please her. It's what she'd always insisted he call her, but it didn't please her. Not with the distance she felt between them that hadn't been there last night.

He pushed to his feet. "I need to get the paperwork to the appropriate parties. I'll call you if anything goes wrong."

"Okay," she said, standing with him, searching his face, but his expression was blank, his jaw set. She wanted to apologize, but wasn't sure what to say, and he was already headed to the door. Maybe he didn't want her to apologize. Maybe...

He hesitated at the exit, and she held her breath, but when she thought he would turn back, he left without another word.

Meagan willed herself not to move, not to go after him. She had a lot of footage to edit, and she needed to check on the contestants herself. She would not go after Sam. She would *not* go after Sam. She sat down again, rested her elbows on her knees and put her hands to her head. Sam was making her crazy.

SAM WAS PISSED, and he wasn't even sure why. He'd left Meagan's room this morning determined to see her again, to find out where this thing with her was going. He'd gone into that break room, with exactly that purpose in mind. Instead, she'd warned him of her vow to keep things between them to one night and that hit him hard.

She had some deep need for control, and from what he could tell, she had her reasons. Her parents had controlled her and were still trying. Apparently, she thought he would want to do the same, and the only way she could control what was happening between them, what was uncontrollable, was to simply shut it down. Maybe that was for the best. He knew better than to mix business with pleasure. He needed to focus on the show, on security, on Kiki. Both he and Sabrina had agreed that Kiki's comments to Josh meant she planned to turn Meagan's show into another bonus opportunity for herself. He just had to prove it before Kiki made it happen.

His mind shifted back to Meagan, to her naked and perfect in his arms the night before, to her rejection today. His stride lengthened, his pace quickened. He was acting like a fool, pursuing a woman who didn't want him. He needed some space, maybe a bar and another woman, only he had too much work to do. And who was he fooling? He was too into Meagan to want anyone else.

He unlocked the door to his truck and slid inside, before pounding the steering wheel. When his cell rang, he said, "Talk to me," noting Josh was the caller. Loud music ripped through the phone. "Where the heck are you?"

"Kiki took a group of the contestants to the eighteen and over club on the corner two blocks south of the hotel," he shouted. "They're performing, Sam."

"Without studio approval or security?" Sam asked, and he could already smell the trouble.

"That's right," he said. "I told her the studio could be sued if anything went wrong. Sam. She said Meagan approved this."

Sam cursed. "Where are they?"

"Club Z and they're filming—"

The line went dead.

Sam punched Meagan's cell number into his phone. She didn't answer. Of course not. She was going to make him come to her. He shoved open his door, and started for the building, angry and feeling as foul as a soldier dodging a sniper—who, in this case, happened to be the woman he couldn't get enough of.

That's when he spotted Meagan running toward him. "Sam!" Apparently, she'd gotten a phone call, too. "Sam." She screeched to a halt in front of him, her chest rising and falling with exertion. "Sam, I—we—"

"I know," he said. "Josh told me. Let's go."

"Josh? What? What's happening? Is something happening with the cast?"

She didn't know? Had she followed him to the truck for personal reasons? Was she here *for him,* not the bar problem? He didn't get to ask. He quickly updated Meagan.

"Sam, this is bad," she said when he'd finished and they'd climbed into his truck. "The studio's liability if someone gets hurt is bad enough. But we have sponsors that expect a family show. If there's the slightest piece of footage of someone doing something they shouldn't, we could lose them. And that could be the end of us."

"And," he said, "it gets worse. Kiki told Josh that you approved this."

"What? No. Please tell me no, Sam."

"I know the truth," he spoke softly. "I have your back, Meagan."

# 13

THOUGH SHE'D MADE SAM WAIT for her to run inside the production building for her purse and phone, having learned her lesson about leaving them behind, the short ten-minute ride from the studio to the hotel felt like a lifetime to Meagan.

The instant Sam put his foot on the brake, stopping next to the valet stand, they were both already shoving open their doors.

"Which way to Club Z?" he was asking the young kid he'd palmed his keys to, as Meagan came around to his side.

"Two blocks to the right, then another right, you can't miss it," the valet told him.

She and Sam were walking before the kid ever finished speaking. "I can't believe Kiki is there, and brought cameras. How did she even manage that, Sam? I mean there would be release forms and legal issues."

"You know the answer," he said. "She planned this in advance."

"Right. She did. She had to have done just that. I

can't let this go, Sam. I have to let Sabrina know, but Kiki's going to say I'm behind it. I can't believe this is happening."

They approached the club, loud music banging through the door, and a long line of people waiting to enter the building. Sam motioned her toward the door, then chatted with the bouncer, leaning in close to the brawny man guarding the entryway, to say something that was, apparently, worthy of entry.

Sam reached for her hand and pulled her in front of him, into a narrow hallway. His touch sent a shiver of awareness up her arm, and all over her body. Her mind went back to the break room, to the kiss, to his departure. She'd gone after him, and not because of this mess. She hadn't known about any of this. She'd followed him because whatever had made him leave so abruptly, whatever had made him withdraw, she had this horrible feeling, it was going to haunt her in ways she had yet to discover—and didn't want to. Because like it or not, she *liked* him. He mattered.

One of his hands settled on her waist as she pressed her way toward the crowded bar, which appeared to have two levels, and balconies above the dance floor. There were also stairs leading to a lower floor.

Sam pushed in next to her, his body framing hers, branding her with memories of the prior night. He bent down, his lips near her ear. "Let's stay close. I don't want to lose you in this chaos."

She turned instinctively, and suddenly, her mouth was inches from his, his breath warm on her cheek. "Yes. Okay." Their eyes locked, and all the shadows in the world couldn't mask the connection that crackled between them. She was so alive with Sam.

He leaned in closer again, to talk to her, the spicy scent of him rushing over her—she so loved the way the man smelled. "Shall we try upstairs or down first?" he asked.

"Hey!" Someone screamed. "Some television show is filming downstairs. We have to go downstairs." A rush toward the lower level followed, bodies flooding past them.

Meagan and Sam shared a look of inevitability. They knew where they were going now, and clearly, they weren't the only ones headed there. He motioned with his head and drew her hand in his. A lot of maneuvers, bumps, and her feet getting stomped, and soon they made it down the stairs to find a huge area blocked off around a stage. Four of Meagan's dancers were performing, with cameras rolling. No director, no Meagan—just Kiki and everyone who hadn't been busting their butts in the editing room.

Anger rolled inside Meagan and she pulled away from Sam, charging forward. Meagan had been cautious around Kiki and her corporate connection for too long. She and her assistant were going to do a little dancing of their own.

SAM'S MEN HAD STEPPED UP to the plate, which was one piece of good in a lot of bad. He owed Josh a heck of a lot of kudos. The stage was well secured, the safety of the cast ensured as well as it could be, considering the circumstances. But there was no way to get the dancers off the stage, in the middle of a routine, without making matters worse.

Holding his position, Sam stood a few feet from Meagan, watching the heated exchange between her and Kiki, and noting the moment she broke from the argument to speak to Jensen, the show's host, and then to one of the cameramen.

She then stood alone inside the ropes, arms crossed in front of her chest. She all but screamed annoyance, louder in Sam's mind, than the music thrumming against every particle in the place. The dancer's routine ended, and another started, and still Meagan didn't move. Clearly, she'd decided to let this continue.

Sam made his way over to Josh, who'd texted his position. Sam ended up almost directly across from Meagan, who was staring at the stage.

"We breaking this up or what, boss?" Josh shouted over the music.

Sam could see the tension in Meagan's body, despite the distance between them. Whatever had gone down between her and Kiki wasn't good. Not that he'd expected it to be good, but he had a strong feeling that whatever had happened was worse than bad.

Suddenly, Meagan started walking toward the back of the stage. Sam cut Josh a sideways look. "Hold everyone right here. If anyone so much as breathes in another direction, I expect you to be on them."

Josh gave him a two-finger salute, and then Sam was moving toward Meagan. He rounded the back of the stage and found a long hallway with a restroom sign, which was the only place Meagan could have gone.

He found her at the end of the narrow hallway and

to the right, leaning against a wall with her head back, her eyes shut. For a moment, with her unaware of his presence, he took in the sight of her.

Petite and sexy, her long dark hair brushing her shoulders, he was so in tune with Meagan. He'd always had a connection to this woman. They had always been headed toward each other.

Everything male—hot and protective—screamed inside him, and pushed him into action. There was no hesitation, no thought of rejection, of her not needing him right now, because he knew she did.

Sam went to her, and before she knew he'd joined her, his hand gently cupped the side of her face, comforting her, while the other hand rested against the wall near her chin.

Her head lowered, eyes fixed on his, hands settling on his chest. "Sam." She breathed out the word, and there as if relief there, like she was glad to see him.

"Talk to me, sweetheart. What happened? And why are you back here alone?"

"Just needed to think a minute. I'm handling this all wrong. Kiki and I argued. I threatened. She threatened. She won. She swears I signed a release for tonight along with some other forms I signed. She had to have snuck it in and I missed it."

"Is that possible?"

"I don't know. I told her I want to see the forms. But she says that if I go to Sabrina she'll say she warned me about tonight's potential liability ahead of time. I screwed up, Sam. I can't even pull the dancers from the club because she said I can't. Because *she said,* end of story. I okayed things in my contract I shouldn't have.

I can be removed if I'm a detriment to my own show. I can't stop Kiki."

"I can," he said. "I'll—"

She leaned in and pressed her mouth to his, the softness of her lips, the willingness of the connection, making him instantly rock hard.

"Don't," she whispered a moment later. "Don't protect me, Sam. I don't want to drag you into her line of fire. I won't let that happen. Just…just kiss me."

His arm slid around her. "I'll do both." He slanted his mouth over hers. She moaned and leaned into him, her hands gripping his shoulders. Something wild sprung to life around them—the club, the music, the desire so long bubbling between them—igniting in the seclusion of this one tiny spot, their escape in the midst of chaos. And the acknowledgment that they'd lied when they said they'd never kiss like this again.

Sam deepened the kiss, drinking her in. He knew even though she'd said "one night," that she wanted another as badly as he did. His hands were all over her body, her hands were all over his—under his shirt, caressing his skin—scorching him to the point that he was ready to take her right here and now. And he wanted to.

He wanted to forget everything—he had forgotten everything. He should be focused on his job, but he was here, ready to rip her clothes off, damn thankful he could trust Josh to handle things elsewhere.

He stopped and pulled back to look at her. "You accuse me of wanting control," he said. "Yet you steal it from me at every turn."

"You can have it," she panted. "I don't want it."

She reached for his jaw again, and he kissed her,

tasted her, but there was something in her words, in her face, and he pulled back again, tenderness colliding with passion. "You aren't letting her defeat you. I won't let you."

"Stop talking," she ordered, sliding her hand down the front of his pants and stroking his cock. "Why are you always talking?"

Why was he talking? He palmed her backside and melded her to his shaft, claiming her mouth again, running his hand roughly over her breasts, pinching her nipples.

"Sam—" she moaned.

"Oh, yes—*Sam*." The cold female voice that wasn't Meagan's froze both of them in place. Kiki.

"No," Meagan whispered. "No."

"Oh, yes. Yes, yes!" Kiki laughed. "I am here, and boy, what a show."

Sam cursed under his breath, fully intending to handle this mess, so Meagan didn't have to. But he should have known that Meagan's moment of weakness when he'd found her in this hallway, was just that. And it was over now. In true Meagan form, she faced Kiki, obviously refusing to let her get the best of her. But before Meagan could say anything screams bellowed through the air. "Fight! Fight!"

Meagan took off running past Kiki, Sam behind her. They rounded the corner to discover the crowd surrounding the stage, where the dancers had been performing only minutes before. Now, a shoving match appeared to be taking place.

Meagan's family-approved dance show was turning into a version of female fight club and that meant sponsors could be lost. And so could the show.

# 14

MEAGAN WAS ON the stage in a heartbeat thanks to Sam, who lifted her up and then jumped up behind her. And thanks to Sam's staff, not only were the observers being held at bay, the fight was somewhat under control, as well.

Josh, and a female security person employed by Sam, were holding two contestants apart—Tabitha and a petite brunette dancer named Carrie White. Meagan had thought Carrie was fairly timid, but considering the clear mark down Tabitha's face, she wasn't so sure anymore.

Tabitha was fighting Josh, trying to get to Carrie. "You better watch your back!" Tabitha yelled at Carrie. "I'm going to make you pay for scratching me."

"Enough!" Meagan yelled. "If either of you touches the other one again, you're off the show." She eyed them both. "Understood?"

Carrie quickly nodded. "I was just defending myself. She jumped on me, Meagan. She jumped on me and… I swear I was defending myself."

Jensen, the tall, blond New Yorker, stepped forward. "It's true. Tabitha jumped on Carrie."

It didn't take Meagan long to put two and two together. Tabitha and Jensen had been flirting on set. And since Jensen was defending Carrie, instead of Tabitha, it was a good bet that there was some sort of jealousy thing going on between the girls.

Kiki rushed onto the stage, conveniently after the fight had been derailed. "What happened?"

"They didn't belong here, is what happened," Sam said and motioned to Josh. "There's a back door by the bathrooms. Let's get everyone out that way, and make it snappy. As in yesterday."

Fifteen minutes later, the dancers were heading in the direction of the hotel as Meagan and Sam followed. "You okay?" he asked, touching her arm to draw her to a halt.

"As okay as I can be considering what happened tonight."

"I called Sabrina," he said.

"What? When?"

"A few minutes ago." He held up his hand. "And before you get mad—"

"I'm not," she said. "I'm not. I know you're trying to help, Sam. I know and I appreciate it. But I don't want to drag you into this and endanger your career, and I feel like I already have."

"It's my job to protect the studio," he said. "I'm working on a documentation trail that backs up my concerns about Kiki. I'll handle this, but in the meantime, you have to keep her from doing any irreversible damage to the show."

"I'm trying. I am desperately trying. What was the outcome of the call?"

"Sabrina thinks a lot of you and this show, but she has powerful people she answers to and big money at stake. I have full authority to investigate Kiki but she is well connected and she's been praised for saving the network from several disasters. I'm fairly confident they were manufactured disasters. She's clearly been rewarded for her actions in some way, shape or form, and she's just as clearly after the gold now. We have to tread carefully."

"If she's that powerful then tonight might be the end, Sam. If that fight makes the tabloids then it could already be the death of our sponsors."

"Then get more."

"It's not that easy for a new show, Sam."

"All right. Then let's think this through. You want the cameras rolling in the house because you want to feature the real lives of the contestants while they traveled this journey."

"Yes, but this isn't what I had in mind. I thought it would be kids getting nervous about performances, their dreams and desires. Their inspiration. Not threats, fights and exploding water pipes."

"So, not real life, then."

"Yes, real life."

"You're too close to this show emotionally," he said. "Step back and think of it like you did when you were producing a news program. Surely, you were battling competitors all the time for top stories."

"Yes," she said. "We were."

"Then do that now. Stop thinking about the show

like it's a dream. Save that for the celebration when it's a hit."

She considered him a moment and nodded. "You're right. You are absolutely right."

"Okay, then," he said. "Us Special Ops guys are all about damage control. My first thought is that what happened tonight, despite Kiki's manipulation and mishandling, was raw and very real."

"Not in a good way," Meagan argued.

"Reality means real—and that isn't always pretty. That fight evolved from the pressures of competition, more than anything else. I bet you can do something with that to make it a powerful episode."

His words sparked a few interesting ideas in Meagan's mind. "You know, now that I'm thinking about this with some distance, I think I can. I could even do a press release and frame the fight the way I want it framed. I can send it to the sponsors and promise them some preview footage before I air a show around tonight's events."

"Perfect," he said. "Hell, give Kiki credit. Praise her to your staff. If you spin tonight into something brilliant, you deflate her efforts to make you look bad. Which means tonight becomes a win for the show."

A slow smile slid onto Meagan's lips. "Oh my God, you are the one who's brilliant. I love you, Sam."

The words dropped heavily between them, out before she could stop them. She could barely breathe because…she might actually be falling in love with him.

"And here I thought I'd be lucky just to get you to like me." His voice was soft, his gaze hot.

Meagan didn't know what to say so she did what

she always did with Sam. She picked a fight. "I won't if you do things like tonight. You distracted me from a critical situation and had me making out in the club."

"No, I didn't."

She blinked. "What? That's all you're going to say? No, you didn't."

"You were beating yourself up, and searching for a way to feel something other than defeat. You used me to do that, and I was helpless to resist, though I shouldn't have been. I should have been focused on my job. So *you* distracted *me*."

"You're blaming *me* for distracting *you* from *your* job?"

He smiled. "Exactly."

"You distracted me," she said. "*You* distracted *me*, Sam."

"Seems we have a mutually distracting impact on one another."

"So we can't…we have to stop doing things like tonight."

"I want to kiss you."

"No."

"*Yes*. I do."

"*No*. You can't. We can't, Sam." Her chest tightened because the realization washed over her and she couldn't selfishly ignore it at Sam's expense. "Kiki is going—"

"I don't care about Kiki."

"I do. We have to."

"Let's walk," he said abruptly, turning toward the hotel, clearly not happy with her.

Meagan's stomach clenched. Her chest got even tighter. The same feelings she'd had back in the break room. She wanted him to understand, yet she didn't want him to understand at all. She was more screwed up over Sam than ever.

"That's it?" she asked, falling into step with him. "Let's walk?"

"What do you want me to do besides walk?" he asked. "Pull you against the wall and kiss you again?"

Yes. Oh, yes. Please. She grabbed his arm and brought him to a standstill. "You're making me crazy, Sam. I don't know what to do here."

"Right there with ya, sweetheart."

"Sam. Please. Even Sabrina is cautious about Kiki. Sabrina! She's powerful. She's one of the executives. I'm afraid that I'll drag you to the unemployment line with me if this goes badly."

"No," he said. "That's not the problem. I'm trying to get through this with you. You're trying to find a way to do it without me. There's a difference. A big difference." He started to walk again. She didn't. She stared after him, all that emotion in her chest balled so tightly, she could barely breathe. She wanted to go after him, she wanted to dispute his words, make him understand. But he wouldn't understand. She'd figured that out about Sam.

He wasn't an arrogant jerk. He wasn't a control freak. He had a whole lot of hero in him. He'd tell her it was okay, that he wasn't risking his job, to be with her. And that mattered to her. He mattered to her. She had to let him go.

He was right though. Rather than using her smarts, she'd been letting her emotions get involved when

dealing with Kiki, and everything to do with this
show. That ended tonight.

EARLY THE NEXT MORNING, Sam was awake and thankful for the coffeemaker in the room. He might be a
soldier at heart, but he'd never been a soldier who de-
nied himself thick, black hardcore caffeine when he
needed it.

He finished off a cup, with one thing on his mind.
Meagan had let him walk away the night before. Again.
Damn, he'd never been a glutton for punishment before.
This was unfamiliar, uncomfortable territory, and he
had to get some space, to get his head clear. Setting the
mug aside, dressed in his jeans and a T-shirt, he was
ready to finish the deal for the house and get his hands
dirty securing the property.

Around the hotel, Meagan was too close for comfort.
Where just knowing she was a few doors down had him
climbing the walls, and right out of his skin.

He stepped into the deserted hallway, everyone still
in bed, when he was surprised to hear a contestant's
door open and then quietly shut. Sam frowned and soon
came face to face with Carrie.

"Oh, I...I...didn't think anyone would be up yet."

"I see that," he commented, noting the rolling suit-
case behind her. The kid couldn't be more than eighteen or nineteen, maybe twenty. "Going somewhere?"

Silent tears started to stream down her cheeks, and
Sam knew exactly what he had to do. "Come with me."

A few seconds later, Meagan's door opened. She was
still wearing a pair of Mickey Mouse pajamas, with her
hair sticking up wildly, and looking more sexy than he

could imagine any one woman looking. And when such an appearance could not only get a guy hot, but make him smile, inside out, he was as hooked as a bee on honey. Sam knew right then, he couldn't hide from what this woman was doing to him, no matter how he tried.

The instant Meagan saw Carrie, her eyes widened, all signs of sleep slipping away. She hugged Carrie, her eyes meeting Sam's. She motioned them inside.

The kitten met Sam at the door, meowing loudly. Sam fed the hungry little beast, and then went for the coffeepot, knowing that Meagan was running on limited to no sleep. By the time the pot was brewing, Meagan had Carrie sitting cross-legged across from her on the bed, spilling her story.

"She hates me," Carrie was saying. "Absolutely hates me."

"Competition can be brutal," Meagan said. "But everything worth having is worth fighting for. And you know what? The things you have to work the hardest for, are the ones you appreciate the most. The question is, do you want this bad enough to fight for it? Your packed bag makes me wonder."

"I want to dance," she said. "I don't want to fight with Tabitha."

"So you don't want this."

"That's not what I said!"

"You aren't willing to fight."

"I am."

"Just not Tabitha."

"She's the meanest person I've ever known."

"Until you meet the next one like her," Meagan pointed out. "There are tons of Kikis in this world."

Sam took a seat nearby, across from the bed. Meagan's eyes found his an instant before she added, "Listen, Carrie. Real life isn't always pretty. Everyone isn't going to be nice to you, and everything isn't going to come with a shiny pink bow on top. You can't let people like Tabitha steal your dreams, make you give up."

Sam took in those words, took in what she was telling him indirectly. She had a dream and she was scared of losing it. He knew that, but hearing it again wasn't easy. She had baggage she had to deal with, and there wasn't room for him inside her life until she did—if she ever did.

"I sprained my ankle last night," Carrie announced. "It's bad, Meagan. I hid it but it's getting worse." She laughed bitterly. "I'd rather the curse would have gotten anything but my ankle."

"There is no curse," Meagan said. "And a sprain can be wrapped and medicated. You have ten days before your first performance. Or, you can use that and Tabitha as reason to quit. Your choice."

"I don't want to quit. I don't. But—"

"No buts," Meagan warned. "I'm going to get tough with you now. In or out. Fight or give up. You choose."

"You really think I can do this?"

"It doesn't matter what I think," she said. "It matters what you know. But for the record, you wouldn't be here if I didn't believe in you."

Carrie flung her arms around Meagan's neck and hugged her. The unfinished business between Meagan and him thicker than the coffee he'd made in his room.

"I'm going to fight. I'm going to beat Tabitha and win this competition."

"Good," Meagan said. "I can't wait to watch it happen."

More chatter followed, and some coddling of the kitten, before Carrie returned to her room to sleep as long as she could before rehearsals, which had been pushed back, after the nightclub incident, until noon.

Sam made to leave, as well.

"Sam, wait," Meagan said, her hand touching his arm, heat scorching, his cock thickening as if she'd just invited him to join her in bed.

He held the door open, not about to let rumors fly any more than they probably were. He also wasn't about to tempt himself into kissing her how he'd wanted to ever since he'd walked into the room.

His gaze met hers, and he could read her expression, read the "I can't" in her face. "I met with my crew last night and we did a press release that also went to the sponsors. One of the sponsors called me immediately and expressed how thrilled they were with the buzz the show was getting. After that, Kiki happily took credit, and I was happy to let her."

"Good," he said. "I'm glad it worked out."

"Me, too," she said, and hesitated, as if she wanted to add something else.

Sam continued waiting, wanting to know what that something else was, his heart racing. This woman really was making him crazy.

Finally, she said, "I…I left my phone and purse in your truck."

"Right," he answered flatly, his pulse slowing. "Your phone and your purse. I'll have it dropped off." He didn't wait for a reply. He left with absolutely no question in his mind, that once again, she had purposely let him go. It was a habit she couldn't seem to break.

## 15

A WEEK LATER, MEAGAN was pacing the stage in the auditorium where the first live show would take place in two days. Two short, too quickly approaching days and too many days away from Sam. Oh, he was around, but he wasn't really around, not for her, that was. It didn't matter that it was for the best, that it was the right thing to do to protect him. She missed him.

She raked her hand through her hair, her stress level at its highest. There was an electronic short in the stage's lighting system, thus sound checks had gone horribly, and the hot band that was set to perform for the big premiere had cancelled. Their lead singer had laryngitis.

The "cursed" and "nightclub" episodes of the show had run two nights in a row with huge ratings, but the live show was the true test. Could the dancing part of the equation pull in ratings? There were plenty inside the studio who doubted that, thus the contestant house had been incorporated into the concept of the show.

"We snagged Mason Montgomery," Kiki announced, rushing down the center aisle. Mason Montgomery being a popular new singer who'd just hit the charts. "He'll be here and he's excited to perform."

Meagan let out a relieved breath. "That's great news." To Kiki's credit, and Sam's for his suggestion, ever since she'd given Kiki credit for the nightclub episode, she'd actually seemed to care about the show.

"Are we moving into the house tomorrow or what?" Kiki asked, drawing to the edge of the stage, next to the judges' table, hands on her hips. "We need to get organized."

"Negotiations are still underway," she said. "But I hope so. I'm expecting word any minute."

Kiki grimaced. "Look. I know you hate the reality, club-fight stuff, but our ratings are off the charts. I want this show to make it as much as you do. We need to do something spectacular to ensure the dancing gets an audience. We don't have time to make that happen in the house this week."

Meagan's cell phone rang, and she eyed the number. "That's Josh now." Josh. Not Sam. She'd barely seen, or talked to Sam since Carrie's visit to her room. She was shocked at just how much she missed that banter.

She flipped open her phone. "Hey, Josh."

"We're a go, but Sam wants you to drive out and give us a final thumbs-up before we get everyone out here."

Meagan ended the call, eager to see the house and move in. And yes. Eager to see Sam.

"I NEED A SCREWDRIVER," Sam yelled to one of his men from under the kitchen cabinet of the contestant's house.

"One screwdriver coming up." The tool landed in his outstretched palm, and Sam went completely still.

Meagan. Meagan, so close her leg was touching his. Slowly, he eased his head out from under the cabinet to find her squatting beside him. Little brown wisps of hair floating over her brow. He loved her hair—how it felt, how it smelled.

"Your man is apparently MIA, since he's nowhere to be found," she said. "And I wasn't aware you did plumbing."

"I don't," he said, sitting up and leaning against the cabinet. "One of the kitchen cameras is acting up, screwing up the entire link to go live. I'll need you to outline where the private areas are besides the obvious ones. There won't be many, still, we don't want any peep shows."

She nodded, then surprised him by sitting down on the floor herself, her back to the island kitchen so that she faced him. "The entire electrical system at the auditorium is out of whack. An electrician is working on it. I think I'm beginning to believe in the curse."

"The ratings don't seem to be cursed. They've been good so far."

"A blessing for sure," she agreed. "Nothing is going as I expected but it still seems to be okay."

He rested his hand on one knee and stretched out the other leg. "Just because it's not how you envisioned it doesn't mean it's not good."

She studied him. "Like you, Sam. You aren't what I expected."

"So you've told me."

"You've been avoiding me."

No one could accuse her of beating around the bush. "I've been busy out here."

"And avoiding me."

"And avoiding you," he conceded. "Yes."

"Why?"

"Isn't that what you wanted?"

"Apparently not."

He arched a brow. "Apparently not?"

"I think I miss arguing with you."

"Think?"

"Okay I do. I miss arguing with you."

"We'll have plenty of opportunity when we both move in here."

"So what's the scoop? Can we be in this place tomorrow?"

"Looks like. I just want to walk you through the camera setups." He started to get up.

"Sam." She spoke softly, his name packed with so much emotion that it might as well have been a shout.

"Yeah, sweetheart?"

"I miss you."

"You made this decision."

"I really was just trying to protect you."

"I don't need to be protected."

"You're sure about that? Because I'm not."

"Completely."

"But—"

"No buts about it."

"Then…about that kiss I said no to…" She crawled toward him and pressed her mouth to his.

SAM WASN'T SURE WHAT screamed louder—his desire for this woman, or the warning to stay away from her. His hand slid to the side of her face, his lips brushing hers. He told himself to tread cautiously, that he was getting emotionally attached to Meagan, and while he had no doubt she was truly into him, he wasn't sure, that emotion had anything to do with him, no matter how much he wanted to be, that he wasn't simply her escape. Whatever she'd been feeling in the hallway of that club a week before, she was feeling now, too.

But things had changed for him—or at least had become more clear. He liked Meagan. He liked her a lot. And even though Sam was on unfamiliar ground, he wasn't one to run from whatever came his way. He damn sure wasn't about to start with Meagan. He had every intention of finding out what was between them, beyond one heck of a lot of smoking-hot attraction.

She pulled back slightly, her breath warm, her mouth still deliciously near and tempting. He knew in his gut that no matter how much he wanted her naked and in his arms, she was hiding—from her true self and from him. He wasn't going to let her do that.

"Why tonight, Meagan?" he asked. "Why tonight and not last night? Or the night before?"

A door slammed. That they'd been alone this long was a miracle. Now there was no time to talk to Meagan, and make his position clear, though he fully intended to. Just like he didn't run from things, he didn't play games, or talk in circles.

"Let's check out the property," he said, before they were interrupted. He quickly brushed his mouth over hers, silently reassuring her that he welcomed their intimacy. He then pushed to his feet and pulled her with him.

"Sam—" she started, looking surprisingly vulnerable, an emotion he hadn't often seen in her.

Josh entered the room. "We're fine in… Oh, hey, Meagan. I bet you're glad to finally be moving in."

"Very," she agreed and exchanged some small talk with him, before Sam had Josh finish up under the cabinet.

A few minutes later, they'd reviewed the in-house cameras, and were standing on the porch. "If we walk up the beach, I can show you where we set up cameras."

"There are cameras on the actual beach?"

"That's right," he said. "It allows us to ensure we don't have any trespassers, and it gives you some extra unscripted footage to weed through."

"That's more than I could have asked for," she said. "I know this must be a huge change from the army for you, Sam, but if it's any consolation, you're good at what you do."

"I aim to please," he said, leaning on the railing. "I'm focused on the future, not the past. I'm simply not one to linger on what I've lost."

"But an injury took your career," she said. "Doesn't that ever make you angry?"

"Sure. I was angry when it happened. I was angry as hell. But it happened, and I can't change history. You climb inside yourself, duke it out, and move on. And is this where I think I'll end up? Only if I decide I have real value, if I feel I'm contributing. And right now, I'm pretty okay with just helping you succeed."

Surprise overtook her expression. "Sam."

"This matters to you on some deep level that I know I don't understand. But I want to. And things that matter to people the way this matters to you, matters to me." He realized something that had been in the back of his mind for a while. "What are you having trouble letting go of, Meagan?"

She inhaled sharply. "Why would you ask me that?"

"Because I can sense there's something you cling to, something that you carry around like a concrete block," he said. "And because I want to know what makes you tick."

He half expected her to withdraw, but she didn't. Instead, still facing him, she pressed her palm against the railing he was leaning on. "This first season is like standing on a rug, certain it's going to be yanked out from underneath you. For me, I feel like this is it. If this show doesn't make it, I need to reevaluate and figure out where I fit, if I fit, in this industry." She paused. "Did you say let's walk? I think walking would be good right now."

They headed down the beach. Dim lights illuminated their path, as they strolled in silence laden with unspoken questions and untouched passion.

"You asked why I kissed you tonight," Meagan blurted, turning to him.

"Tell me," he encouraged, not surprised by her directness, or how much it appealed to him.

"I like you, Sam Kellar."

She couldn't have said anything more perfect. It was exactly what he'd been thinking in the kitchen. "I like you, too, Meagan Tippan." He stepped close to her, wrapping her in his arms. "So where does that leave us?"

The lights around them flickered, and someone shouted, with footsteps running along the beach. "Apparently," she said, "with nowhere to hide."

Good, he thought. Because he wasn't going to let her hide. She'd opened the door to let him inside her life, and he was coming in, armed and ready to get to know every intimate detail.

"Let me finish up here, and then we'll…talk."

She smiled, mischief in her eyes. "Good. I'm up for a good argument."

"Me, too," he assured her. "That is, as long as we get to kiss and make up."

# 16

MEAGAN WAS NERVOUS. Nervous! How insane was that? But she and Sam had taken their connection to a new level tonight. Meagan had no idea she was going to kiss Sam while they were on the kitchen floor, but she was glad she had. She was so tired of controlling everything around her, and, despite her spent nerves, it was almost a relief to have her wild desire for Sam become a fact.

Her cell phone rang, and she quickly stuck her headset in her ear and hit the answer button without taking her eyes off the road. She was driving back to the hotel with Sam in his vehicle behind her. She'd been trying to reach Kiki or Shayla all evening with no answer, and that worried her.

"Hello."

"Why do you sound like you want to bite my head off?"

She laughed instantly at the sound of Sam's voice, which was a testament to how much she needed the distraction that was this man. To think she'd believed it would be a bad thing. "I didn't know I did. Sorry. I've been trying to reach Kiki and Shayla and I can't. Considering her track record, silence from Kiki still twists me in knots."

"And you want to let her live in the mother-in-law house with you?" he asked, reminding her of the decision she'd shared with him earlier in the evening.

"I need her under thumb, where I can watch her."

"If she's at the second house, she'll be under my thumb and...on second thought, I think she should stay with you."

"Yeah, I bet you do," Meagan said. "I'm not so sure Josh would agree. He seems to get all hot and bothered when she's near."

"Josh's no fool, or he wouldn't work for me. He knows what Kiki's really about," he said.

She sighed and went back to the prior subject. "I can't believe they aren't taking my calls."

"Don't assume the worst," he said. "I think we should get your mind off of it."

"How do you propose we do that?"

"By talking about something else. What's your favorite color?"

"Are you serious?"

"As a heart attack. So—what is it?"

She laughed softly. "Fine. It's red."

"Why?"

"It's bold and daring like I dreamt of being when I was growing up in a small conservative Texas town. What about you?"

"Orange."

"Like the Texas Longhorns?"

"Only a Texan would turn orange into Texas Longhorn burnt orange," he said. "I'm talking California orange—a new day's sun burning over the ocean. I was born here, you know. Those sunrises were one of the things I missed when I was gone. Us soldiers see more dirt and grunge than we do oceans and sunrises."

Sam was a soldier, a Special Forces soldier. Who knew what all he'd seen, what he'd lived. "Your job was risking your life," she said, feeling a heavy dose of perspective. "It makes all my worries about television and ratings so shallow."

"Soldiers fight for right and wrong, and for freedom. This show, and the kids chasing their dreams, is part of that, too. The land of opportunity, where you dare to dream, and make those dreams real." His voice softened, husky and male, and oh so alluring. "Don't start turning yourself into a villain, Meagan. You'll steal all of Kiki's fun. Which is a bad subject, so let's get back to the American dream. It makes me think of apple pie, which I love. Do you know how to make one?"

She laughed. "I know how to buy one at the bakery, which is far better than anything I could ever bake. Though I make a mean pan of Kraft mac'n'cheese, which is, I assume, because I follow instructions well. It's one of my favorite late-night dinners."

"Excellent choice. I'm fond of it myself."

The drive flew by as Sam drilled her with random questions that had her laughing and eagerly waiting for his own answers in return.

It wasn't until she pulled into the hotel parking lot, and found a spot, with Sam whipping in next to her, that she realized two things. She hadn't heard from her staff, or even tried to call them during the drive. And she was suddenly nervous again about being alone with Sam. Which was nuts. She'd already slept with Sam. She'd done naughty things with Sam in his truck. But she'd also convinced herself those adventures were just that. Adventures. Until tonight. Tonight "things" had become a relationship for her and Sam.

She shoved open her door to find Sam already approaching, and before she could let her nervousness get the best of her, he pulled her into his arms and kissed her. A hot, passionate, reassuring kiss.

"I had to do that before we go inside and the insanity of whatever waits for us steals you away from me."

"Do it again," she ordered, and when he did, she decided there really was more to Sam than bossy alpha male. She really liked the way this soldier took orders.

THEY DIDN'T HAVE TO AGREE to be discreet, they simply were, and Meagan liked Sam all the more for intuitively knowing what was necessary. And somehow, riding the elevator from the garage to the lobby, with him beside her, looking straight ahead, not touching her, only stoked her desire. They'd switched elevators and rode to their private floor. The elevator dinged and Meagan found herself casting Sam a sideways smile. He arched a brow at her all-too-obvious "I want you" look, the heat in his expression saying he was feeling exactly what she was.

The doors slid open, and he motioned her forward. Her smile faded fairly fast when she found a large group of her crew and almost every dancer in the competition sitting around on sofas and chairs, with food and beverages, in the common area. Several cameras were rolling, one of which singled out her and Sam.

"Off of me," she told her cameraman. "You know how I feel about that."

"You're no fun, Meagan," the cameraman shouted.

"I'm not supposed to be fun," she commented. "I'm the producer."

"That's why they have me," Kiki said, lifting her glass.

Meagan gestured to her, and Kiki sighed heavily before arriving at her side. "Before you say anything, we had no brilliant footage ideas for tonight, so we *all* decided to just chill out and talk, and hope for something good to happen."

Carrie and Tabitha had Jensen sandwiched between them. The two giggled and hugged him. He was smiling from ear to ear.

Meagan and Sam exchanged a worried look. She sought out her director. Shayla's expression was one of concern, as well.

"From fight to ménage," Shayla whispered. "If that isn't good television, I don't know what is."

"Or another fight, and a lawsuit," Sam said softly, giving the crowd his back.

"Exactly," Meagan echoed. She wasn't about to stand by and let Tabitha and Carrie end up in another argument, but she chose her words cautiously with Kiki. "While I reluctantly appreciate what you're trying to do for ratings, we need to tread cautiously."

"This is darn good footage, Meagan," Kiki said in a low voice. "This little romantic drama will make them crazy-popular."

Meagan bit back her first reaction, which was disapproval. "In that case, we don't want them to get kicked off the show for poor behavior. We need to get them to go relax and go to bed. We're moving to the house early tomorrow."

"Well, that's good," Kiki said. "But I really dislike the dance part of this show."

"That would be the entire show," Meagan responded.

Kiki snorted and addressed the group. "We're moving into the new house tomorrow, everyone," she called out, "so be ready to leave at the crack of dawn. Time for bed." There were lots of moans and groans, and chaos that followed, but the announcement got everyone moving.

Meagan and Kiki chatted with DJ and Ginger to ensure they were prepared for their lead roles in the move, and then in the new house. Sam and several of his staff ended up in a powwow of some sort by the elevator, and as much as she didn't want to notice, she could tell the instant Sam stepped away. Once all the contestants were in their rooms, Sam positioned several of his people on the floor to ensure no one snuck out. Sam then disappeared with Josh in tow.

In her room, Meagan fought the empty, disappointed feeling she had. She was alone. As in, without Sam, and she admitted now just how much that wasn't how she wanted this night to end.

For the first time in three years, Meagan had not only let someone into her life, she'd let another alpha in. That should terrify her, and scream of a mistake. She'd always chosen the wrong men. But Sam didn't seem wrong. Nor was he some alpha control freak. Sam was...

well, he was Sam, who managed to somehow make being tough and strong so darn alluring and perfect. And now that he was in, she wanted him here, with her. She wondered if he was thinking the same thing, if he wanted to be here. And if he did, why wasn't he?

She laughed that off, knowing all too well, it wasn't as if he could just walk up to her door and come in without creating talk. She might have caved to the impossibility of staying away from Sam, but she still didn't want to paint a bulls-eye on his chest for Kiki. Kiki seemed to be into the show though. Meagan had researched the other programs Kiki had been involved in and this was the first with huge ratings out of the gate. Her hope was that Kiki would believe this show's success was a bigger feather in her cap than its demise.

She shoved aside thoughts of a failed show, and headed to the bathroom, for her surefire comfort ritual of a hot bath. She was about to step into the tub, when her cell rang.

She rushed to grab it from her purse, saw Sam's number and smiled. She flipped the cell open.

"And now you know why I kissed you by the car," he said, without a hello.

She returned to the tub and sank down into her favorite jasmine-scented bubbles. "Now I know."

"Where are you?"

"In my room. You?"

"On my way back to the hotel from the property. We had a problem with some reporters who managed to find their way out there, but it's under control. They're gone."

"Wow," Meagan said. "I don't know whether to be

frustrated or excited that the show is getting so much attention."

"I'll handle the frustrated," he said. "You just be excited."

Warmth filled her. "You keep making me want to say thank you, and I'm afraid it will go to your head."

"Sometimes you have to live dangerously."

"Hmm," she said. "I would rather do that in person."

"Alone time isn't going to be easy to come by."

"Yeah, I know. That kind of stinks."

His voice softened. "Do you wish I was there now?"

She was done being cautious with Sam. "Yes. I do."

"I do, too. You want to have phone sex?"

She laughed. "I'm not into phone sex, Sam."

"Have you ever had phone sex?"

"No."

"Then how do you know if you haven't tried?"

"I don't want to try. Though I can certainly imagine all kinds of things I'd do to you if you were here now."

"Like what?"

"Sam, I'm not—"

"Humor me."

"Fine. I'd be in charge. I'd make you undress—as in completely. I wouldn't undress. Then I'd drop to my knees and lick—"

"Stop," he ordered. "Bad idea after all. I'm driving, and you're going to make me crash."

"Or you don't like the idea of me being in charge?"

"You want to play dominatrix, bring on the leather and whips. Just as long as you remember whatever torture you dish out, I plan to return tenfold."

"Promises, promises."

"That is a promise. You can count on it."

She was so counting on it. And when they hung up, after talking about everything from Kiki to the odd *ménage* possibilities between Tabitha, Carrie, and Jensen, Sam's brother and their relationship, and even how much Meagan had often wished for a sibling, she was still counting on it.

She couldn't wait to test Sam, to discover her inner dominatrix and see just what his "tenfold" promise would reveal.

# 17

THE NEXT DAY CAME and the arguments over who got what room, while impossible to avoid, were easy to predict. When it looked as if Tabitha and Carrie might end up rooming together, Meagan vetoed it, in spite of Kiki's approving the pairing. Ultimately, Carrie would be crushed if she lost this competition, and Meagan saw the writing on the wall—Tabitha would happily manipulate Carrie to ensure that Carrie failed and she succeeded. In the midst of this, Meagan reviewed the locations of cameras, and a list of house rules.

When it was all said and done, what Meagan hadn't predicted was the somber mood that would overtake the group as they settled into the house. One of them would be gone in only a few days, eliminated at the first live show.

Prior to rehearsal at the studio, Meagan and Sam had managed a few steamy stares with, frustratingly, no hope of acting on the crackling energy anytime soon.

Per Sam's instructions, at nearly ten that night, Meagan called him to report their approach to the house. He was determined to greet her, and the contestants, at the house, to personally ensure he prevented any problems for their first night's stay.

The contestants filed up the stairs, with moans of aching bodies, and a need for bed. "I'm going, too," Kiki said from the doorway. "I'm dead to the world."

That left Meagan and Sam in the foyer of the main house, staring at one another. Suddenly, her tired body was alive and alert.

"And here I thought we'd never manage to be alone tonight," he said, for her ears only.

"If only it were so easy." She had this bad feeling about combusting into flames from wanting this man so badly. She motioned to their surroundings. "I have this terrible fear that this is an alternate universe, and once we step outside it, the real world will erupt around us." And just like that—as if she had jinxed them—a female scream came from the top floor.

"You had to say that, didn't you?" Sam asked, even as they charged toward the girls' side of the house.

They found Tabitha and her assigned roommate—a redhead named Jenny Michaels—on top of the bed. "Mouse! We have a mouse."

The hall filled with females, followed by shouts from the guys, who were also charging up the stairs.

Sam used a stern "soldier in charge" voice, and ordered them all to their rooms, and boy, was Meagan glad he did. Truth be told, she didn't have that kind of energy.

And even if she had Sam alone, tonight was not the night for them. She wanted to be everything she could be, when she was with him again.

After they'd calmed everyone down except for Tabitha and Jenny, who were insisting they move to another room, Sam stopped Meagan in the hallway for a private chat. "You know the best answer to catching a mouse, don't you?"

"If you mean a cat," she said. "Samantha's not quite ready for the job. She's as small as a large mouse right now."

"Ah, but we don't need Samantha," he said. "I found an adult cat today."

"Really? Samantha's mother maybe?"

"Maybe. Anyway, I say we put him to the test."

"Bring on the mouser, so we can try and get some sleep."

He motioned to the girls. "I'll leave you to the...fun, while I fetch Mel to help."

"Mel?"

"I didn't have the heart to call *him* Meagan, despite the fierceness so like your own. But a man—even the tomcat version—can be sensitive about a name. And we need him feeling manly right now."

She laughed and waved him off. "Go get Mel, then."

Mel turned out to be a big hit, adored by everyone in the house, and reveling in all the praise. Meagan and Sam promised to adopt a friend for Mel the next day, which Sam vowed he'd name Meg. Eventually, Sam escorted Meagan to the mother-in-law house, where they walked up the wooden steps of the rectangular deck, and were, at least, semi-alone.

"Well," he said, resting his palm on the doorframe above her head as she rested her back on the door. "I guess this is where I say goodnight."

"Yeah," she said. "I guess so."

"I take it goodnight kisses are off limits."

She barely quelled the urge to push to her toes and take that goodnight kiss. "Probably not the most discreet thing to do."

"You do know this is killing me," he said. "I've been thinking about our 'almost' phone sex all day."

She laughed and bit her bottom lip. "Yeah?"

"Yeah." His eyes darkened and he pushed off the door. "I better go before I decide not to. Or do something someone will see, and which you'll hate me for later. And I'm not calling you when I get to the other place, or I might change my mind and come right back here."

He stepped away, as if he couldn't quite get himself to turn. "Night, Meg."

"Mea...gan."

"Okay, sweetheart," he said, his voice low. "Meagan." And then he turned and walked authoritatively away, all broad-shouldered and muscle-defined, and totally confident. She sighed and entered the house to find Kiki leaning on the kitchen counter, sipping from a coffee cup.

"Oh, hi," Meagan said. "What's up?"

Kiki smirked. "Nothing," she said. "Nothing at all."

But her look, her tone, didn't say nothing. It said something.

Knots formed in Meagan's stomach. Had she just put Sam back on Kiki's radar? Meagan said a quick goodnight to Kiki, thankful it was an easy escape. How was she supposed to do a good job if she was always so worried about her assistant. If this show had a season two,

Meagan was negotiating Kiki out of the contract. That would be a deal breaker. In the meantime, it was critical that Meagan decide how best to protect Sam without destroying what felt like a really good thing.

OVERNIGHT, MEAGAN REALIZED that Sam would never back away from the potential threat that Kiki might represent. She had to pull away from him again, and she wasn't sure he'd forgive her for that. Still, she resolved to do what she hadn't. Take action. She started her search for a new agent immediately. As much as she valued the importance of control, she hadn't been embracing it at all. Taking action was the only thing that kept her distance from Sam in place.

It was early evening when she arrived at the house for the night. After changing into jeans and a T-shirt, she headed to the contestant's house, where everyone was having dinner. Meagan made her way to the kitchen to snag a soda right when Sam came in with a small pet carrier, holding a beautiful white cat.

The instant Sam's eyes met hers, she felt that familiar punch of awareness in her chest. "Hey, sweetheart. How was your day?"

"Productive," she said, and a torment, she added silently. Staying away from Sam when she didn't want to was incredibly hard.

"I'd say mine was too, considering what I have here." He set the carrier on the island counter.

"She's gorgeous," Meagan said sliding a finger inside the bars to stroke the friendly animal who purred loudly. "A perfect friend for Mel."

"We had great timing with this one," he said. "She had to be rescued today or—"

"Don't say it," Meagan ordered, stroking the animal through the bars. "I'm just glad we can give her a home."

"Her name is Meg," he said, a teasing glint in his eyes.

She laughed. "I deserve that, now don't I?"

"She's beautiful!" Ginger called from the doorway, "DJ! Come here!"

It wasn't long before Meg was carried to the other room, and smothered with attention, leaving Meagan alone again with Sam. "It appears Meg is a hit," Meagan said.

"Yes," he agreed. "Meg most definitely is a hit."

The air all but crackled around them. She couldn't help but stare into the man's too-blue eyes. Could she be falling in love with him?

She wanted to tell him her concerns about Kiki, but he was stubborn and macho. He'd insist he didn't need protection.

"Sam—"

"Look at Meg go!" Ginger shouted, and before Meagan could find a way out of it, she and Sam were herded into the living room. They joined the group as everyone talked about how excited but scared they were over the live show the next night, but declared Meg and Mel good luck charms and the "curse" officially gone.

Sam escorted her to her door again, and she felt wildly out of control. She had to change the dynamic between them and she didn't know how. She was juggling so much, trying to make everything turn out right for everyone, for him.

"Stop looking at me with those crazy-blue eyes of yours. It makes it impossible to resist you."

His lips twitched slightly. "Good," he whispered, and before she could stop him, his lips were softly touching hers. "Sorry, but it was killing me not to touch you. Now go rest. You look exhausted." Then he was sauntering away again, just as sexy as ever.

"Stop telling me I look exhausted. That's not nice."

Sexy male laughter floated on the beach air. The sound mingled with the scent of his spicy cologne, and wrapped itself around her like a warm blanket of pure lusty need. She was never going to get any sleep. Worse. She was never going to resist Sam. The only way to avoid him would be to tick him off. She really didn't think she had that in her.

"THE STUDIO CALLED," Kiki said, in the kitchen the following morning. "The ratings for last night's pre-live show were off the charts. The cyberworld is buzzing about the Tabitha, Carrie, Jensen triangle."

"That's great news," Meagan said excitedly, filling a coffee mug. "That should ensure great ratings for tonight's show. Did June say anything about how Sabrina reacted?"

"Oh, Sabrina's assistant didn't call," she said. "Sabrina did."

Sabrina. Sabrina had called Kiki. Her stomach knotted. Sabrina didn't make those kinds of calls. June did. So maybe Kiki and Sabrina were tighter than she thought, than even Sam thought. She tried not to let that worry her. Kiki really was behaving. Meagan was meeting with a potential agent today, a big name with a lot of power, who swore he could negotiate her contract for next season now. Things were going to be fine. Things *were fine*.

"And you're right," Kiki agreed. "Last night's ratings should ensure tonight's. That's exactly what Sabrina said, too."

Meagan didn't miss Kiki's gloating. Kiki gloated. Meagan knew this. It meant nothing. Although, it was hard not to be paranoid, considering what she had found out about Kiki.

"Great," Meagan said, hoping she sounded sincere as she dumped some French vanilla creamer in her cup. "I'm going straight to the theater to be sure we're ready for tonight. I'll see you at the rehearsal studio."

With the contestants long gone, and Kiki with them, Meagan opened her car door to find a bag of chocolate and a note that read "someone I know told me that chocolate is the only medicine for nerves, Sam."

She inhaled, emotion welling inside her. She grabbed the bag and opened it, climbed in her car and started eating. Who cared if it was seven in the morning? She needed this chocolate, and a part of her was starting to acknowledge how much she might just need Sam. Sam, who'd somehow managed to be there for her, without ever taking over her life, without once interfering where he wasn't wanted.

Meagan pulled her car onto the highway, telling herself not to eat the entire bag of chocolate. Chocolate was her weakness, and apparently, so was Sam. Neither seemed like a bad thing right now. In fact, both were pretty darn good.

It WAS EVENING, twenty minutes until *Stepping Up* went live for the first time, complete with an audience. And every time Sam had seen Meagan, she'd seemed more frazzled.

When he eventually located her backstage, she was in conversation with a tech guy, and it wasn't going well.

"You yelled at two of my dancers right before they have to go on stage," she said. "Okay, you're under pressure here, we all are, but that doesn't mean you can be rude."

"I'm trying to fix the lights before the show starts," he said, tapping his watch. "I have eighteen minutes. Seventeen by the time I finish this sentence."

"Meagan," Sam said, joining them. "Can I review a few last-minute security points before the show starts?"

She whirled on him. "Is there a problem? A security issue?"

"Everything is fine," he assured her, promising himself he wouldn't kiss away her fears no matter how tempting the idea. He was crazy about this woman— completely, insanely crazy for her, like he'd never imagined he'd be over a woman. "Walk with me."

"Sam—"

"Walk with me, Meagan," he repeated, adding a bit of push to the words he was sure would get him yelled at, especially when he turned and strolled away, with the assumption she would follow.

She did and he stopped behind a curtained-off area, much like a small room, used to enclose supplies.

He grabbed his phone and dialed one of his men. "Electronics problem on set. We could use your magical touch right about now, Rick." He hung up. "Listen, Meagan." He ran his hands down her arms. "You need to take a deep breath and ease up a little."

"Sam, please don't—"

"Don't what?" he asked. "Worry about you? Ask what I can do to help? Care enough to be here with you, instead of somewhere else?"

She blinked at him and then pressed her hand to her face. "I'm sorry. I'm just…" She looked at him. "I'm a wreck. I swear this show has made me this way. I was never like this in the newsroom. You were right. I'm too close to this."

"In a few minutes, what will happen, is what will happen. Whatever that final product is, embrace it and call it a success, Meg."

She paused, considering his words, and then to his surprise, pushed to her toes and kissed him. She smiled at him and then disappeared back onto the stage.

Sam's lips turned upward, his blood running hot for Meagan, who was driving him to the edge, he wanted her so badly. And though he was certain their time out of bed was working in his favor, helping him to get to know her, keeping her from hiding behind sex, he was damn ready to strip her naked and have his way with her. Or *her* have her way with him. He really didn't care, as long as the end result meant they were together.

Tonight couldn't arrive fast enough as far as he was concerned. In fact, tonight seemed a perfect time for pleasure in celebration of the success he was sure the show was going to have.

It was the prospect of holding Meagan, and making love to her, that led him through the next several hours of the show—including the tight security needs of a Pop star—with that smile remaining on his face. That was, until the last fifteen minutes of the show, when the bottom three dancers were announced.

Sam stood across the stage from Meagan, his eyes locked intently with hers. Derek, the host, called the first name. A dancer named Rena took her place next to Derek. The second name… Tabitha. Sam couldn't say he'd be sorry to see her leave. But it was the next name that set the place into a purr of shocked "ohhhhs." The final name was Carrie.

Sam watched as Meagan's face paled. Yes, he knew she had a soft spot for Carrie, but beyond that, Meagan was a smart cookie. She was bound to be thinking the same thing he was. What were the chances that both Carrie and Tabitha would end up in the bottom three without some manipulation of the results?

# 18

MEAGAN FELT SICK when Carrie's name was called. She did see Carrie as the underdog, which she'd always felt a bit herself. But then there was the coincidence factor. Had the judges been persuaded formally or informally to put Carrie's and Tabitha's names on the bottom three?

Kiki stepped to Meagan's side, digging her fingers into Meagan's arm. "We can't lose Carrie or Tabitha. Please tell me we aren't about to lose Carrie or Tabitha. We need them for ratings."

Relief washed over Meagan. Kiki hadn't played with the outcome of the judging. This second guessing Kiki thing was distracting her more than she thought.

"The first contestant that's safe is…" Derek said, "Tabitha."

Tabitha squealed and rushed to the bleacher-style seating where the other nine safe contestants were sitting. She flung her arms around Jensen's neck. Carrie looked sad and disappointed, and suddenly Meagan felt as if she were on that stage with Carrie, about to hear her fate. She felt guilty for that, knowing this was emotional for the other candidate, Rena, as well, but it was Carrie whose moment Meagan was in.

"And the final contestant who is safe tonight is... Carrie!" Carrie burst into tears right along with the girl who'd just found out she would be the first to leave the show. Instead of rushing to safety, Carrie turned to her and hugged Rena. Meagan watched Carrie walk with the ousted dancer, talking to her, comforting her, and knew she was right about Carrie being a nice person.

Derek wrapped up the broadcast and the aftermath followed, the celebration and tears backstage. Meagan spoke to the celebrity judges and put fears of contestant tampering aside. These were people who took their roles seriously. The performances had been the deciding factor, and Carrie and Tabitha had spent too much time focused on Jensen, rather than on practicing, to come out on top.

When Meagan's team, with Sam and his men following closely, arrived at the contestants' house, they'd all vowed there would be a midnight swim. By the time they'd all quickly changed, a delivery of gourmet strawberry cupcakes arrived, donated by a famous chef who hosted a show on the same network. Everyone dug into the treats, even Rena, who seemed to find the indulgence welcome.

Meagan stood in the kitchen, watching the crowd, feeling sad that Rena was leaving, but relieved that the girl had been offered a Broadway audition before they'd ever left the theater. Meagan wanted to create dreams that came true, not crush them.

"It could have been me saying goodbye tonight," Carrie said as she joined Meagan in the kitchen.

"You're right," Meagan agreed. "It could have been you. Stop focusing on Tabitha and Jensen, and focus on dancing."

Carrie leaned on the island counter. "I know. Believe me, I know. Dancing is everything to me, and not only did I almost quit the show, I almost let silly distractions ruin it for me, too. I've lost track of my priorities."

Distractions. Priorities. Meagan had allowed herself to be distracted by Sam, but somehow, he'd helped her move forward, not held her back. It was this Kiki distraction that was destroying her. She was at the point where she needed to just let the cards fall where they would with the show. She was working hard. She'd landed her new agent today. She had to learn that some things were out of her control. Like her strategy for Sam. She didn't want to let down her guard and be with Sam, only to find him the true loser by associating with her.

She shoved aside the worry, at least, for now, and challenged Carrie to succeed. "So what are you going to do to make sure tonight doesn't happen again?"

"Practice and focus." Her voice tightened with emotion. "Thank you for talking me out of leaving. I've gotten several lifelines now. I'm not foolish enough to think I'll get another."

"Good," she said, picking up a cupcake to take to Rena. "I'll hold you to that."

"Carrie!" came a shout.

Meagan shooed her away. "Go enjoy tonight. Tomorrow it's back to work, harder than ever."

Carrie grinned and took off to the other room.

Meagan sighed, and with a growling stomach that

had been treated to nothing but chocolate that day, she snatched a cupcake from a tray for herself and scooped decadent icing onto her finger. In the next moment, Sam showed up, his heated gaze zeroing in on her finger in her mouth. "I see I've been missing more than I realized."

Meagan laughed, wondering how it was that Sam always had such interesting timing.

"Tabitha!" Carrie screeched abruptly from the other room. "That was so mean."

Meagan and Sam both raced toward the girls, but it was too late. Rena grabbed a cupcake, and smashed it into Tabitha's face. A snowball effect ensued, and before Meagan knew what hit her—as in a cupcake or two or three—there was icing flying everywhere.

"Enough!" Meagan shouted, standing in the middle of it all. Another cupcake bounced off her chest.

Sam echoed her order. "Enough!" he yelled. A cupcake bounced off hit him in the forehead.

Meagan burst out laughing. Seeing rough and tough Sam plopped in the head with a strawberry cupcake was just too much on too little sleep.

He cast her a grumpy look in reaction to her amusement. Meagan liberated one of the last cupcakes from a contestant's hand and scooped some icing. She wasn't even going to think about the furniture or the floors. She'd be damned if she was wasting a gourmet cupcake, when she hadn't eaten today.

Once she'd finished her cupcake, and was starting on a second, the frenzy died down, and Meagan's cell phone, tucked in her pocket, began to ring. With sticky fingers, she pulled out her cell and eyed caller ID.

Meagan's gut clenched. This wasn't about cupcakes. It was about ratings, and since the call wasn't going to Kiki, but to her, her stomach clenched tighter. Maybe she only got the bad news calls, and Kiki got the good? She answered, listening to Sabrina deliver the verdict. And it wasn't bad news, not bad news at all.

Meagan grabbed Sam's arm and had him boost her up on top of the coffee table to shout out. "Top show of the night, people! Top show of the night!" At least in preliminary ratings, and that was fine by Meagan. Joy ensued, and Kiki of all people jumped on top of the table and hugged her. Sparkling grape juice sprayed Meagan and Kiki's already strawberry-flavored skin.

"Midnight swim!" someone hollered. "Midnight swim!" A mad rush for the door followed.

Meagan stood where she was and tried to revel in the moment. But next week's ratings would be the real test, and next week's booted contestant might not get a Broadway audition.

"Whatever you're thinking, stop," Sam ordered, standing beside the table. "Tonight is about success."

"What about the contestants?" she asked. "I have to watch out for them."

He grabbed his phone and made a call, in which he asked someone to see to her gang. "Josh will keep an eye on them," he told her and held out his hand. "Tonight, you're mine."

She glanced down at Sam from on top of the table. at his hot-and-hungry stare, she felt certain he was prepared to clean the icing from her entire body. And boy did she believe she could do the job on him. For days now she'd wanted this man, for days she'd wondered if it was unquenched desire for him or something more. For days now she'd been stressed, worried, confused. She'd felt as if the world were spinning out of control.

For tonight, what was wrong with being on top of the world? Okay, she was on top of a coffee table, but with a cake-covered, gorgeous army guy about to carry her away to a private place, she believed she could do anything. She had a hot show and a hot man. If that was a curse, bring it on.

She slid her hand into his.

SAM HAD PLANS FOR Meagan, a celebration of her success, that led them down the beach, off the grid of the cameras, to a secluded area where he'd pitched a tent and set up a lantern inside.

Meagan laughed the minute she saw the tent.

"I thought I'd show you how a soldier roughs it on the beach." He motioned her inside, and she disappeared through the open zipper. "And you and I get privacy we wouldn't get at either of the houses."

"Champagne?" she asked, as he joined her on the inflatable mattress.

"Unless you prefer the sparking grape juice you're wearing as perfume? Derek was right when he said those kids are crazy."

She laughed. "They're excited."

"As they should be," he said, and popped the top on the bottle and filled her glass. "Congrats on your ratings." His mouth brushed hers. "You taste like strawberries. I think I just decided I love strawberries." And yes, he'd said love. He was falling in love with Meagan. He'd never been in love, thought it wasn't in his cards.

And he was probably a fool to choose a woman sure to kick his ass a hundred times over, but then, Sam never ran from a challenge. And Meagan was more his kind of challenge than any he'd known in a very long time.

She inhaled on his words, as if she'd understood the discreet message. Softly, she breathed out his name. "Sam." Her fingers curled on his cheek, and for long seconds stayed there. The air was thick around them, electric and hot, until she pressed her lips to his. "You... taste like strawberries, too."

"I taste like you," he told her, leaning back so she could see his expression. Then he slipped a glass into her hand. "Drink up. You deserve to celebrate."

She crinkled her nose and downed the drink. "Always the bossy one, aren't you?"

"Hmm," he said, emptying his glass and scooting to her side. "You seem to like me being bossy, like I do you, at least sometimes."

"Only because it hasn't gone to your head," she said, letting him ease her to the mattress. "The minute it does—"

"You'll put me in my place," he said, framing her face with his hands. "I know. Believe me, I know. I like that about you, too. But do you know why you keep letting me take control?"

"I'm sure you'll tell me," she commented dryly, but not without a rasp of desire in her voice.

"Aside from trusting me," he began.

"When did this become about trust?"

"Are you saying you don't trust me?" he asked, sliding her shirt up to her stomach and kissing the delicate skin he'd revealed.

"I didn't say that."

He caressed her narrow waist, her hips. "So you do trust me?"

Her expression softened. "I do," she whispered. "I trust you, Sam. Very much."

The confession took him off guard, warmed him. "I'm glad," he said, resting his hand on her belly. "Not so long ago, I wasn't so sure you ever would."

A smile tugged on her lips. "You kind of blasted into my life like a bolt of lightening. The minute you arrived, I felt your presence."

"I know the feeling."

He would have lowered his head to kiss her then, but her fingers slid into his hair. "Do you ever feel out of control, Sam?"

"When I'm not with you."

"I'm serious," she said.

"So am I, sweetheart. I've never had a woman twist me in knots like you can."

"I don't mean to do that to you."

"Then stop pushing me away. Let me inside, Meg. Really let me in."

"I don't want to push you away," she said. "But—"

He kissed her. "Then don't. Just don't. Be with me, Meagan."

"I am, but—"

He kissed her again, a long stroke of his tongue against hers, before repeating, "Let me in, Meagan. Let go of just enough control to give me room inside your life. Everyone has to let go sometimes."

"If everyone has to let go of control sometimes, when do you let go?"

"Whenever you say you want me to."

She searched his face. "That easily? Just like that."

"Sweetheart, your definition of control and mine are two different things. You don't think I've given it up, but I have."

"What does that mean?"

"It means I not only can't stop thinking about you or wanting you," he admitted. "I don't even want to try."

"I feel the same way," she said. "I do. I—"

His mouth came down on hers, hungry to claim her. Finally, she'd stopping fighting him, stopped pushing him away. This had never been about the chase with Meagan. It had been about this, about how good she felt in his arms, how good they felt together. He knew now that all those years that he'd sworn he wasn't a relationship man, had been because he hadn't met Meagan.

She moaned, her tongue meeting his, caressing his. Sam rolled on top of Meagan, feeling her delicate curves beneath him, his hand sliding down her hip, beneath her backside, to arch her against the thick ridge of his erection.

She murmured his name, pleading with him. He pulled back to stare down at her, to search her face. "I never believed one night was enough. Or two, or three, or—"

She leaned up and captured his lips with hers. "Me, either," she said.

A wild frenzy of touches, kisses, and undressing followed. Until she was beneath him, naked and perfect. Until he was buried inside her, memorizing every inch of her beautiful, heavy-lidded stare. He saw the trust there, in her, but he knew instinctively, it was still fragile, still far too easily shattered.

## 19

MEAGAN HAD DONE just what Sam had suggested. She'd let go of control, let herself say what she felt, let herself just be with Sam. Even now, after they'd dressed again, her in her bikini and Sam in a pair of swim trucks he'd worn under his jeans, she sensed the newfound intimacy between them. A closeness that had nothing to do with sex, and everything to do with making love.

Meagan sipped from her glass. "Thank goodness I told everyone to sleep in tomorrow," Meagan said, the bubbles tickling her nose. "I have a feeling my head is going to pay for the sugar and champagne in the morning."

"There's a twenty-four-hour diner a mile up the road," he said. "We could walk it."

"With cheeseburgers?"

"I'm pretty sure any diner has a cheeseburger."

"Then count me in," she said, agreeably, reaching for her sandals and T-shirt as Sam did the same. That was when her eyes caught on the scar above his knee.

Her hand went to it, and he froze a moment, his shirt

half over his head, the action telling her the injury was more of a sensitive spot than it was a physical injury.

"Does it bother you often?" she asked, as he pulled his shirt on. She remembered the way he'd rubbed it when they'd been in his truck the week before.

"I deal with it," he said, repeating what he'd already told her.

She knew that all too well, thanks to a knee injury of her own that flared often. It hurt. "Will you tell me about it?"

"I was on a covert mission in enemy territory," he said. "It wasn't the bullets that got me, but the days without treatment. By the time I was back at camp it was a mess. I almost lost it."

She could barely breathe thinking of how bad his leg must have been, and how devastating the outcome. "You can't tell me that doesn't mess with your head, Sam. You act like it's nothing, but it is."

"I had months of rehab to get my head right."

No one just got their head right that quickly. A horrible thought hit her. He hadn't dealt with his leg. He was going to eventually wake up and reject this new easy life, and her with it. She pulled her hand back from his leg, suddenly feeling burned, certain this thing with Sam was going nowhere good and not sure why that upset her so much. Why couldn't this just be about sex anymore? She began to move away from him.

He grabbed her hand, gently holding her beside him, when she wanted to dart away. "Whatever you're thinking, I can tell it's not good. We're talking about *my* leg, and you're the one withdrawing and I don't get it." His eyes narrowed. "Am I damaged goods, Meg? Is that the problem?"

Her eyes riveted to his. "No. Oh God, no, Sam. It's not like that. Your leg—if anything the scar is sexy and you're more man than any I've ever known. And that's exactly why I must seem silly to you, worried about dancing and ratings, when you've been off saving lives and protecting our country. Coddling me must be—"

He slid his hand into her hair. "I never coddle you. How could anyone ever coddle you? You're way too tough for that. And there's nothing silly about a dream." He stroked her cheek with his thumb. "We've had this conversation. Dreams are what soldiers fight for. And your dream is personal to me now. You're personal to me."

"I believe you mean that. I do. I see nothing but honesty and directness in you, Sam, and that matters to me. It's been part of what has made you so hard to ignore. Probably why I didn't want you to talk to me and show me what I already sensed was there. But you had your life stripped away by an injury." She looked away, unable to keep her eyes on him. "I know from things you've said to me that you weren't ready to leave the army. You planned on that life being a career for you. And here you are, in the middle of all this super-ficial glamour."

"And with a woman I really care about."

"Sam," she chastened. "I can't…you have to under-stand that I…" Her voice broke.

"Don't want to count on me if I'm not going to be here," he said, accurately filling in the blanks. "Who let you down, Meagan? Who did you count on who let you down?"

Her lashes lowered, the confessions on her tongue, unspoken—of a dream of dancing, of a family who'd said her injured knee was proof she'd been on the wrong path.

"You don't have to tell me," he said gently. "Not now, but I hope sometime soon you will. You're right. The network isn't for me long term."

Her gaze lifted sharply, a knife jabbing her right in the chest. "I didn't think so."

"I have a plan. And that plan is probably why I'm okay with where I'm at now and will be in the future. I'll be opening a private security business next year, when several of my former Special Force team opt out of re-enlistment. And my uncle, the one who works for the studio, is our primary investor. He fully intends to pull some of the Hollywood crowd as clientele and even move studio business."

Relief washed through her. Sam wasn't going to run off. Sam was invested in this world, in her world. Sam was Sam, and she liked everything that meant.

"Why are you smiling?"

"I don't know," she replied honestly, but she really couldn't hold it back. She kissed him, and it was a good thing that the diner was open twenty-four-hours because they'd managed to undress again.

Meagan and Sam shifted comfortably on the mattress. "You've been so polite lately," he said. "We haven't fought at all. You've been full of thank-yous."

"You complaining?" she challenged.

"Not at all," he assured her. "In fact, I like the way

you say thank you. So much so that I wonder if I can make you say it now?" He trailed kisses down her jaw, over her neck, until he suckled her nipples, teased them with his tongue and his teeth.

"No thank you yet?" he asked, lapping at a hard peak.

"Not yet," she confirmed. "Right now, you're just driving me crazy."

"Hmm," he said. He suckled again. "I like that."

"I don't."

He raised his head. "No? I'll see what else I can come up with." He palmed her breasts and kissed a path down her stomach, until he was licking her, teasing her, in the most intimate of ways. And just before he pushed her over the blissful edge, before she happily said thank you, she made a vow.

"Just remember. One thank-you deserves another. Your time is coming."

And the low masculine laughter that radiated against her clit, sent her tumbling into release. She'd never had a man bring her to orgasm in the midst of laughter, but then, there were a lot of firsts with Sam. And that made letting go feel a whole lot less scary.

AN HOUR LATER, SAM reluctantly allowed Meagan to dress, but only because of her threat that she'd collapse if he didn't feed her. He had this nagging feeling that as soon as they exited the tent, she'd run from him emotionally. He'd pushed her tonight, taken her from "don't talk so I won't like you" to someplace much more intense, much more long term, and he could see that she was wrestling with that wall of hers—which meant *he* was wrestling with that wall of hers.

They were just stepping out of the tent, into the cool air rising off the ocean, a high moon overhead, and he was looking forward to the diner, when his cell beeped with a text.

Displeased with the news and knowing she would be too, Sam glanced from the message to Meagan.

"I'm not going to get any food, am I?" she asked.

"Depends," he said. "How do you feel about contestants getting to know each other in, shall we say, an intimate fashion?"

Meagan's eyes went wide and she started walking toward the house. Sam immediately caught up with her. "I take it the answer is, you don't like it. So the good news is that Josh broke them up. They weren't happy but he stopped things before they got too out of hand."

"Jensen and Tabitha?"

He cleared his throat. "And Rena."

"Oh my God," Meagan said, stomping through the sand. "This is forbidden in their contracts. Rena has nothing to lose, but the other two do. And Kiki knows it, but I can bet you she's counting on those cameras we have rolling to tell all. How can I convince her that some facade of good ratings based on scandal will plunge within a few episodes and is not security, without turning her against me? *American Idol* and *Dancing with the Stars* didn't build ratings off of who slept with who and who was fighting who."

"Meagan, sweetheart—"

"I believe so strongly that we can't go in this direction, even if the ratings please the sponsors. I shouldn't have been away. I—"

"Oh no." He shackled her wrist and pulled her to face him. "I see where this is going. Don't even start coming up with reasons to make *us* wrong. We are not wrong, Meagan. You are not wrong by taking a few hours off. And you didn't count on Kiki. You counted on Josh— *on me, Meagan*. Josh contained the problem, and he called us the instant there was trouble."

She let out a breath. "I know and I appreciate it. I do. I really, really do." She tugged on him. "But please come on. We have to hurry. I don't want to lose someone I don't have to lose over this."

They took off towards the contestant house and with the beach lights on, it was lit up well enough to rival the Christmas Vacation house. Soon it was easy to see Carrie sat on the porch with Josh by her side, and Mel in her lap.

"Where are they?" Meagan asked anxiously.

"Beach," Josh said, pointing to the water. "They took off when I told them they couldn't share a bedroom."

Carrie nodded.

"I've got this," Meagan told Sam, and she sprinted away.

Sam watched her depart, and leaned on the railing to the steps. He eyed Carrie. "Good thing you entertained yourself with Mel and not Jensen."

"That's what I told her, too," Josh said. "Life is way too short to bury yourself in a popularity contest."

"The show makes it feel like a popularity contest," Carrie said.

"No," Sam said. "The show is about dancing and

so is your future. Don't let anyone convince you otherwise."

She nodded. "You're right. That became crystal clear to me tonight when I almost got kicked off the show. Jensen and Tabitha have families with money. They can go live in New York and try to make it with a dance company. I have a single mom who's a secretary who I want to take care of one day. I can't believe I ever tried to leave because of them. This is it for me. I'm not blowing it."

No wonder Meagan had taken to Carrie. The kid had character. "Good. That's real good, Carrie."

They talked a few minutes about her mom, her life back in Washington, and the mess in the house that needed to be cleaned up before they saw Meagan and the three dancers approaching the house. Looking guilty as heck, Jensen and Tabitha rushed up the stairs without a word.

Meagan stopped beside Sam. "I threatened to send them both home. Hopefully I gave them a reality check. Neither of them wants to get kicked off the show."

The door swung open and Kiki joined them on the porch. "Talk about some great footage for next week. The 'almost sex' incident is going to be gold."

Meagan eyed Carrie. "Can you please go inside and give us a minute?"

"Yes, of course," Carrie said, and toted Mel up the stairs and past Kiki.

The instant the door was shut, Meagan said, "We can't air this or the studio could make the kids leave the show. I told them that won't happen."

Kiki crossed her arms, attitude rolling off her. "They

chose to ignore their contracts. Besides. They didn't break the rules. They almost broke the rules."

"I doubt they thought we would put this on air."

"Why would you say that?" Kiki asked. "Oh wait." She lifted her chin at Sam. "I suppose you did set a bad example by shoving your tongue down Sam's throat. Maybe we should include some footage of you two instead? We're here for the good of the show and the network."

Kiki's claws were officially back out and Sam wasn't waiting for Meagan's reply. He was close to having the evidence he needed to end Kiki's career as a troublemaker.

He held his hands up. "Sorry, ladies, but I have to throw up a stop sign. Since this is a contractual issue, there are legalities involved. If this footage is used and ends those kids' runs on the show, they could potentially sue. I can't release the film without studio approval. If I do, you two can figure out what to do with it." He glanced between them. "You're both welcome to curse me out over a cheeseburger at the diner down the road."

"I'm going to stay here," Kiki huffed. "I have some phone calls to make." She turned and headed back into the house.

Meagan asked, "How about that burger?"

He arched a brow. "I'm surprised you're willing to leave."

"A very sexy man once told me that sometimes you just have to let go."

## 20

IMAGES PLAYED IN Meagan's sleepy haze. Of sitting at the table across from Sam, of sharing a strawberry milkshake, as if the strawberry cupcake icing hadn't been enough. Of celebrating. Of telling Kiki where she stood. And of kissing Sam goodnight in the shadows behind the house. Then she fell asleep with her own hands on her body, wishing they had been his.

"Wake up, sweetheart."

"Hmm." Meagan snuggled into the warmth of the blanket. She was so tired. So very, very tired. And there was this sweet, warm touch she didn't want to end. The scent of Sam lingered around her.

"Meg, honey, wake up."

"Can't wake up. Not yet."

"Please." Light touches tickled. Warmth trickled along her neck, a nibble of teeth on her earlobe. Wow. This felt real. She sat straight up. The blanket fell to her waist, exposing the skimpy tank top and matching boxers to the hungry blue eyes taking her in without one bit of reserve.

"Sam?"

He sat next to her bed, fully dressed, the sun beaming through the window.

"What happened? Did I oversleep? What's wrong?"

"You let everyone have the morning off, so no, you didn't oversleep, but you weren't answering your phone and I started to worry."

Samantha pounced into her lap and purred. Meagan replied with a long stroke of her back. "Oh yes." She remembered letting everyone sleep, but not her phone ringing. She reached for it and noted that Sam had called her at least a dozen times. "I can't believe I didn't hear it." She set Samantha aside. "What's going on? Why are you here?"

"Kiki took Jensen, Rena, Tabitha and some other dancer named Susie to breakfast. After last night, I didn't think you'd like that."

"Oh no." She started to get up. "That can't be good." Sam leaned in and kissed her, his big hand on her shoulder, and her nipples went instantly stiff and achy.

"I sent Josh along for the ride," he told her. "Kiki wasn't pleased. Neither was Josh."

Relief washed over her. "I seem to owe Josh big favors."

"I owe Josh," he said, setting the kitten on the floor and climbing in bed with her. "He's calling me when they head this way. We're alone. In a real bed."

She bit her lip and curled her arms around his neck, no hesitation. She'd been dreaming about Sam all night. "This feels so very naughty, Sam. We might get caught."

"Naughty, which means hot and fast, if we don't want to get interrupted."

"I like hot and fast," she assured him, splaying her fingers over his crotch, and caressing the thick bulge. "And it seems you like hot and fast too." She unzipped him, and slid her hand inside. "You like it a lot."

His fingers wound around her neck. "Not nearly as much as I'm going to enjoy taking my time with you, someplace secluded and private and soon."

"Promises, promises," she said, gently gripping his cock.

He moaned softly.

"You like?"

"Yeah," he said. "I like."

"I'll tell you a little story," she said, caressing the slick, wet tip of his erection, and then nibbling his neck, then his ear.

"A story?"

"Hmm. You'll like this story, but you have to take your pants off first." She tugged them downward, helping him get as gloriously naked as she wanted him, even as he tugged his shirt over his head. Meagan settled between his legs, hand wrapping around his shaft. "Now for the story. This is the story of how I make you say thank you."

And she drew him into her mouth. His hips lifted, he inhaled deeply, and she smiled at the reaction. She suckled and licked and played with him, until he tried to pull away, before he couldn't. She teased him unmercifully. Before long, he was shaking, all that power that was Sam was radiating through him to her. His release came and she took it all, took him to the moment when he sighed in complete satisfaction, when he relaxed.

She climbed on top of him and kissed him, delivering the promise, "The next time you sneak into my bedroom, the punishment will be a hundred times worse."

His hands closed down on her hips, but she pressed away. "One second." She pushed off him and he let her, not suspecting her departure. "I have to go shower before they get here." And she dashed into the hallway, bare naked. Sam had teased her. This time, she was teasing him.

When he poked his head around the shower curtain, he gave her an intense up-and-down inspection. "I dare you to find out what happens when you sneak into my bedroom tonight."

And then he was gone.

NOT EVEN WORRY OVER a battle with Kiki could keep Meagan from being all smiles as she walked into the contestant house to find everyone, Kiki included, cleaning up the strawberry mess from the night before.

Meagan went in search of Carrie. She found her in the kitchen, sweeping up cake crumbs. "I hear you missed the big breakfast meeting this morning."

Carrie snorted. "I'm happy to be part of my own ménage."

"I wasn't aware you had a ménage," Meagan said, trying for a casual tone.

"All I need is Mel and Josh," she said. "They make fine company. Neither of them are overly friendly, and both give a pretty good comfort pet when needed."

Meagan straightened. "What? Josh's been petting you?"

Carrie giggled. "No. Not like that." She patted Meagan's head. "Like that. Like a big brother kind of petting." She wiggled her hips and brows. "Though bring on more, baby. He's gorgeous."

Meagan shook her head and poured coffee into a mug. "You stay away from Josh. He's too old for you."

"I'm mature for my age," Carrie said. "I'm like a twenty-seven-year-old trapped in a nineteen-year-old's body."

"Oh, Carrie, honey, you just hang on to the nineteen-year-old body," she said. "Take care of it and treat it right so you have a long career, with zero injuries." She lowered her voice. "Any idea what this breakfast was all about?"

"Tabitha said Kiki lectured them about getting into trouble, and warned them she was cracking down before they got her fired."

Meagan's brows dipped at the behavior so contrary to how Kiki had acted the night before.

"Yeah," Carrie said, seeming to read her mind. "Sounds odd to me, too." She leaned in closer. "Last night, Kiki was the one encouraging them to, you know, get down and dirty. So now they want me to believe she was scolding them, telling them they were lucky not to get kicked off the show?"

"That part is true."

Carrie shrugged. "Yeah, well, she didn't seem worried about that last night."

The back door opened and Sam walked in looking like sin and satisfaction—her satisfaction. "Speaking of lucky," Carrie said. "I think I've become a soldier kind of girl."

"Carrie," Meagan warned.

"Sorry. Sorry. I'm leaving." She grinned at Sam. "Hi, Sam." Then she took off into the living room.

Sam sauntered over to the coffeepot, real close to Meagan, and filled a cup for himself. "Morning, Meg."

She smiled. "Morning, Sam."

"It is," he said. "Very good. It started when some-one told me a story."

She smiled. "Really?"

"Oh, yeah," he said, whispering in her ear. "I plan to rewrite the ending. You'll like it."

"I liked the original version," she assured him.

"You'll like this one better. Wait and see." He winked. "Tonight."

Kiki appeared in the doorway. "How about seven o'clock tonight, okay?"

Meagan about swallowed her tongue considering what Sam had just said, and she didn't dare glance at him for fear of completely giving away their conversation. "Tonight?"

"For the group movie night you wanted to organize."

"Oh, yes. In-house movie night. Sure. Excellent." She ignored the mischief in Sam's eyes that said there was way more than a movie night on his mind. "I need to watch what we've filmed in the main. I'm hoping for some really good footage for next week's show."

"If you come down to the security house later this evening," Sam suggested, "I can let you view what we have so far."

Meagan tried not to react to the invitation that had nothing to do with film, and everything to do with get-ting her to his bedroom. "Perfect. I'd like to get to the editing booth early tomorrow."

"Hopefully they deliver some fun viewing minus the scandal," Kiki said. "Don't worry, Meagan. I got the message. No more scandal. You want the show to have mass appeal. I get it." She was being so sweet it was downright sticky. "But if the ratings falter even one week, all bets are off. I'm not going down with the ship." She smiled brightly as if she hadn't just issued a threat. "Meanwhile, dinner's being prepared." She eyed Sam. "So, try and stay out of the kitchen, okay, Sam?"

"Absolutely," he confirmed.

Kiki said, still way too brightly, "And they want to watch Freddy Krueger, Meg. I figured I'd pick up some Jason action, too." She disappeared and Meagan really hoped she was talking about the fictional Jason Meyers, not the Jason who was one of the judges on the show.

"Meg," Sam chuckled. "She just called you Meg, and we both know how dangerous that can be."

"I don't know what scares me more," Meagan agreed. "That woman or having to watch those movies tonight which will ensure I don't sleep for a week. I don't do scary."

"I'll protect you from all the scary bumps in the night," he promised softly, his eyes glistening with something deeper than the jest behind his words.

And oh, how easy it would be to buy into the fantasy that he could protect her, and fix everything that might be scary in life. How easy it would be to be the damsel in distress, and Sam, her knight in shining armor. The idea absolutely made her shake inside. She was falling, too hard and too fast, for Sam. What if she lost her show and him in one fell swoop? What if she started relying on him and then he was gone? Suddenly, she was shaking inside as surely as she had shaken in his arms. She had to get a grip on both herself and her situation.

"Alas," she said, trying to sound lighthearted, to hide the wave of emotion consuming her. She'd told him she wasn't. "Movie night is one nightmare I must face alone, though I know it will break your heart to be left out."

His eyes narrowed, his intelligent stare all too aware of her sudden withdrawal, which was why she did what any intelligent woman would do.

She darted away.

IT WAS A DARK AND STORMY night. Literally. As in, lightening, thunder and pouring rain. A night made for scary movies, though Sam and three of his crew, Josh included, had opted for watching sports and the live security feed.

Sam sat on the couch of the security house, one booted foot crossed over the other on top of the coffee table. Josh and two other guys had taken spots in various locales around the room. The game in question was playing on the big screen, the security footage, on a table lined with monitors that Josh had expertly wired days before.

Sam's gaze kept drifting toward the security footage, toward Meagan, replaying her words as he had in the hours since she'd spoken them. He was no fool. She'd run away the instant she could, and he didn't know what to do about it. It was exactly what she'd promised not to do again. How to handle it was the question. Did he give her some space? Did he press her so that she knew he was serious about where this was going? And he was. Every moment drove that point home. He'd never fallen in love, but he knew he was in love now. He knew months ago with their first sparring words.

Meagan screamed at the movie, and Sam found himself grinning.

He wasn't sure if she, or Carrie, would win the award for loudest scream of the night. Suddenly, lightning struck outside and thunder roared. The entire group of movie watchers screamed, and Sam and his men chuckled. Another blast of lightning and thunder, and the lights went out, including the security feed.

"Damn," came several voices in unison a second before the backup generator, hooked directly to the feed, purred to life.

Sam was already on his feet, dialing Meagan, his eyes adjusting to the darkness. The security feed was useless, nothing but darkness and the mumbles of scared contestants. Sam could hear Meagan's phone ringing, but she was too busy trying to calm everyone down to answer.

One of his men passed out flashlights, and Sam turned his on. "I'm headed over there," Sam said.

Josh groaned. "I'll go with you. Sounds like Freddy Krueger and the storm has them in a total panic."

Ever prepared, they grabbed rain jackets from the supply closet, and extra flashlights. They were about to leave when one of his men shouted. "Hold up, Sam man! We have a tornado warning in effect for the next thirty minutes."

Sam cursed and motioned to Josh. "Let's go now."

The instant they were out the door, they were slammed in a downpour that made it seem like the ocean was raining down on them, not the clouds. Sam ran faster, pushing through the wind and over the sand.

Sam was in sight of the porch stairs to the main house in minutes that felt like hours. His cell was ringing, but he didn't dare stop to answer it. The front door burst open, and Meagan appeared as Sam rushed up the stairs with Josh on his heels.

"Tornado warning," Sam said, wishing they weren't too close to the coast to have a basement, like they'd had in the other house. "Get everyone into the bathrooms now."

Screams followed, and to Meagan's credit, she went into action, calm and collected, moving everyone where they needed to be. Kiki, Ginger, and DJ were calm under pressure, herding the cast and crew to safety.

"Funnel cloud on the ground nearby," Josh shouted behind him.

"What's happening?" Meagan yelled, rushing down the stairs toward him in the beam of his flashlight.

He charged toward her. "Bathroom, sweetheart. Go to the bathroom."

Terror flashed in her eyes, the kind that spoke of panic not calm, but she'd shown it to none of the people in her care. He rushed her to the master shower where several other people were huddled, and pulled her into a corner, wrapping his arms around her.

"Sam?" she whispered.

"I got you, Meg," he said, tightening his hold on her. "I got you, and I won't let anything happen to you."

She stared up at him and then hugged him, her cheek to his chest. "I got you too, Sam."

He buried his face in her hair, and he knew in that instant, he wasn't letting her face this storm, or any other, without him, ever again. Now, he just had to figure out how to convince her of that.

# 21

THE TORNADO BRUSHED past them, but it was enough to shake the walls, terrifying Meagan and everyone else in the house. The minute it was gone, Meagan kissed Sam as she'd never kissed a man in her life. He was officially her hero, and she didn't care who knew. To heck with fears of "what if" things didn't work out with Sam. Life was short and that's why she'd chased her dreams, even when doing so was difficult.

She clung to him and then stared into his eyes. "I am so glad you're here, for so many reasons."

"Me, too, baby. Me, too." He ran his hand down her hair.

"Meagan! Meagan!" Carrie rushed in and bent down to hug her. "I can't believe it. I can't believe this really happened."

"We're okay. That's what counts. I need to make sure everyone else is, as well."

Sam pushed to his feet. "Keep everyone inside until I can make sure it's safe, and assess any damage."

"I'm coming," Meagan said. "Carrie, you stay." She got to her feet.

Sam pressed a flashlight into her hand. "I need you to stay. Let me do what I do. Let me get everyone out of this safely."

She inhaled. Damn, he was hot when he was in soldier mode. She couldn't believe she was thinking that, even under the circumstances. She nodded. "Okay."

He started to turn, but she grabbed his arm, unable to help herself, and she kissed him. "Be careful."

"Always" he said before departing.

"It's the curse," Carrie murmured, drawing Meagan's attention. "There really is a curse."

"If everyone is alive and well, this is a blessing, not a curse."

It was only a few short minutes before Sam shouted all was clear. Meg came running up the stairs and into Carrie's arms, and Meagan's stomach lurched. "Samantha! Sam! Samantha! I have to find Samantha."

Meagan took off toward the front door and didn't stop when splatters of rain hit her face. She dashed over to her own house and, in seconds, was yanking open the door. She dropped her flashlight, and darkness overtook her. Meagan knelt down, fumbling for the flashlight. "Samantha! Here kitty, kitty."

Behind her, someone switched on a flashlight. The scent of Sam was unmistakable. "Do you see her?"

"No." Her heart twisted. "What if something happened to her?"

"She's okay. Just scared and hiding, I'm sure. Here, little girl. Come on, kitty." He moved through the house, calling her in various ways. "There she is."

Meagan heard the cat's meow and just like that, Sam became Samantha's hero, too. He scooped her up in his arms and brought her to Meagan.

"Now that my two girls are safe and united, I need to go deal with this mess." He kissed Meagan's forehead and headed toward the door.

And Meagan was pretty sure in that moment, she had fallen in love with Sam. She was scared, she felt exposed. But tonight in that bathroom, she'd made a decision to put herself out there with Sam, to be willing to get hurt.

JUST BEFORE SUNRISE, having spent the past few hours juggling the after-tornado crisis, Sam found Meagan at her house. She was still dressed in shorts and a T-shirt, asleep on the couch with Samantha curled next to her. The remote control lay by her head, and the weather channel was on mute.

The house was quiet, and he assumed Kiki was asleep. Either way, it didn't matter. Kiki knew that he and Meagan were seeing each other. Probably everyone did, at this point. They hadn't been exactly discreet in the bathroom during the storm.

Sam debated moving Meagan to the bedroom, but feared he'd wake her up and then she wouldn't go back to sleep, especially considering Samantha had a way of getting noisy. And Meagan needed rest. She'd already told him she would have to go to the studio that day to edit this week's show. He turned off the television and then settled onto the floor in front of her, back against the couch, stretching his legs out, exhausted and happy to rest his eyes.

He figured he'd steal Meagan away for breakfast when she woke up. Or just make breakfast. With that delicious thought on his mind, he dosed off, able to sleep in the most awkward of positions.

How long he slept he didn't know, but the sun was up when he woke, and he could hear Kiki talking on her phone as she passed by in the hall behind the sunken living area, the setup blocking Meagan and Sam from her view.

"She's asleep in her room," Kiki said. "Right. I knew I had to call. It's a wonder the kids weren't hurt, Sabrina. No. No. Yes. I'm on my way now." The door opened and shut, and she was gone.

Sam frowned. What was that? What the hell was that? He replayed the conversation, and though there was nothing that screamed foul play in the words, the very fact that Kiki was speaking with Sabrina set him on edge. And the tone of the conversation, something about it.

Sam quickly got to his feet, intending to call Sabrina, who he was still briefing about the Kiki issue. He'd interviewed ex-employees who'd worked with Kiki, and found more than a few who might not have spoken up before, afraid they'd never work again if they did, but they would now. A few key people he'd located had since moved on with their careers with enough confidence to help him. He'd been compiling quite the damning file, but for the kind of connections Kiki had, Sabrina kept pressing for more.

"Sam?" Meagan sat up, her hair a wild, sexy mess of light brown silk, her lids heavy, her voice groggy. "What's wrong?"

Even when she was sleepy and barely awake, she worried, Sam thought. "Why do you always ask me that when you wake up?"

She blinked several times, as if trying to clear her head. "Well. Let's see." She was already sounding a bit feisty, he noted with amusement as she continued, "While I'm not beyond admitting that I tend to worry obsessively about almost everything, I think I have ample reason to do so under the circumstances. A tornado, an electrical fire, a knocked-out tooth, and a long list of other problems—all pretty good reasons to worry. In fact, when I list them, I can buy into the curse a lot easier than I'd like to."

He bent down on one knee in front of her. "There's no curse to a show that brought us together, and I'm going to prove that to you before this season is over."

She visibly relaxed, her expression softening. "Promise?"

He brushed a wild lock of sleek brown hair off her brow. "Promise."

"You're making a lot of promises. I hope you intend to pay up."

"Well now," he said, his hand sliding up her leg. "Since Kiki just left, we are alone."

Her brows dipped. "Kiki left? This early? That's odd."

He kissed her, not about to put her on edge about Kiki when it wasn't necessary. He would have the answer to the problem very soon. "It's all fine, Meg. And did I mention…"

A slow devilish grin slid onto her incredibly sexy mouth. "What do you have in mind?"

He set Samantha down on the floor and scooped Meagan up into his arms, Tarzan-style. "I have a story to tell you."

He carried her to the bathroom, stripped them both naked and pulled her with him under the hot water of the shower. They both sighed with relief, and their bodies melded together, tension melting into attraction, into desire.

Sam leaned against the wall, molding her close, kissing her, taking his time to savor her. She was soft in his arms, her breasts full and tempting, her nipples hard peaks against his chest. And he wanted inside her, wanted to lose himself in her, wanted to claim this woman as his own, and wished it were that easy. But he didn't want to lose her, he didn't want to pressure her. And he darn sure didn't want the sex to be her escape rather than an extension of what he felt for her, what he hoped she felt for him.

"I was thinking about a story I want you to tell me," he said, caressing the wet hair from her face. "Are you ever going to tell me *your* story? All of it, Meg. I know there's something you haven't told me. Something that got you here where you are today."

Her fingers trailed over his jaw, his lips, a moment before her mouth brushed his. "Yes. Yes I am."

"Yes?"

Her fingers stroked his chest, his ribs, between their bodies. "Yes." She smiled against his mouth, wrapped her hand around the thickness of his erection. "I'm most definitely going to let you in."

Desire pumped through his body, but he forced himself to slow down his lust, and his need to just lose himself in Meagan. He reached down, and covered her hand with his. "That's not what I mean."

"I know what you mean, Sam. And the answer is still yes. Yes, I'm going to tell you my story. Yes, I want you in my life. And yes, I still really want you inside me right now." She stroked his cock, and he let her this time.

He'd held weapons while being fired at, and he didn't so much as tremble. But then, he'd never wanted a woman the way he wanted Meagan, never felt what he felt now, with her, always with her.

He sheathed himself, his gaze sweeping her breasts, water droplets clinging to her tight rosy nipples. "You're spectacular."

Her hands slid down his shoulders. "Remember that the next time we disagree."

"Have I told you how much I love your ass?" he asked, palming one cheek, and angling her hip as he settled his shaft between her thighs.

One of her hands slid to his backside. "Have I told you how much I like yours?"

He entered her and she gasped. "Sam," she moaned.

"Yeah, sweetheart?" His forehead settled against hers, his hand skimmed her breast, fingers teasing her nipple.

"About last night." Her hand pressed to his cheek.

He moved his hips, fitting himself deeper inside her. "What about it?"

She panted and then breathlessly replied, "I'm pretty sure when we huddled together and kissed in the shower, everyone figured out we're together."

Together. He liked that word. He liked her using it as

a given. "Yeah," he agreed, his cock swelling inside her, need building within him. "I'm pretty sure they did."

"I don't regret it. I don't care that they know." He pulled back to look at her, and she quickly added, "I know we have to be discreet. I need to be discreet, and I'm sure you want to be discreet. But…but, Sam, in that shower, in the worst of situations, when I was completely out of control, you made me feel…safe. You made me feel safe, Sam."

Sam swallowed her confession in a hungry kiss, knowing the trust that it had cost her, how difficult trust was for her to give. And as for the regret she'd mentioned, he was feeling absolutely none, and he intended to demonstrate that fact in a number of creative ways.

At the stove, Sam filled plates with omelets he'd made and toast, before joining Meagan at the small white kitchen table, where she was listening to a message on her cell phone.

She'd dressed in black jeans and a red T-shirt with a V neckline that displayed ample creamy white skin in a tantalizing way. But then, he had a good imagination where Meagan was concerned, and it wouldn't take much to encourage him to drag her back to the bedroom, if he thought she'd let him.

Meagan sighed and set her phone on the table. "Kiki left me a message that she's meeting me at the studio. Something is just strange about her taking off this morning when we had the tornado last night." She waved away her worry. "I don't have the energy to think about what it might be." Her gaze lit on her plate. "Wow. No one told me you're a chef. I'm starving and this looks so incredibly good. Honestly, Sam. I can't believe you can cook. You don't strike me as the domestic type."

"I still have a lot of surprises for you," he assured her, looking forward to showing her just how many. "You'll find us soldiers are a resourceful bunch."

She took a bite of her eggs and swallowed. "So good, Sam. At least one of us can cook. Don't be expecting anything but microwave from me."

"So you've told me," he said. "But I'm not interested in you for your cooking, I assure you." He poured sugar in his coffee.

She set her fork down as if the subject turned her stomach. "I fired my agent and hired a new one who says next season I can pick my own crew. Michael Beckwith, that's his name, said that I could have gotten that to start with if I'd been with him. He seems to think he can negotiate for next season now, not later, based on the ratings. That's good news, right?"

"Yes," Sam agreed. "It's very good news."

But it also meant Sam needed to step up what he was doing about Kiki. If in future she wasn't going to running the show—Meagan's new agent seemed to be all but guaranteeing that—would Kiki go so far as to ruin it and make herself look good by having jumped from a sinking ship?

# 22

In a whirlwind of ratings, chaos and two more live shows, one of which was going on at that very moment, Sam had become a quiet, strong, passionate force in Meagan's life.

She stood backstage, watching yet another megasuperstar perform and awaiting the bottom three results. The cupcake footage had turned out to be a really fun episode that they'd used to contrast with the tornado footage. That had been last night's broadcast. And boy, had it been a show, with massive ratings that had already stirred talks of renewal for another season. Her agent was sure that would happen and he'd insisted they hold off on further contract talks because ratings were the king of cash, not to mention leverage.

Soon, Derek took center stage to read out the names of the bottom three dancers. Meagan held her breath, waiting for the results.

"Tabitha," Derek called for the first time since the debut show, and the audience wailed, some with boos and some with celebration. Tabitha was, by far, a fan favorite. She seemed equally loved and hated.

"Next up," Derek said. "Kevin." Kevin, tall and brunette, rushed forward—a quiet guy not overly well known because he didn't draw much attention to himself.

"And finally," Derek said, "Carrie."

Meagan's heart stammered instantly. Carrie, like Sam, had surprised her, finding a way into her life that was as powerful as Sam's presence, though different. Carrie was the kid sister Meagan had never had. They cut to commercials on the tense moment of the last name, and Shayla's voice came through Meagan's headset, "I really, really hope she doesn't go."

"Me, too," Meagan whispered. "Me, too."

Sam stepped into view across the stage, out of audience viewing range. It was the perfect place; exactly where she needed him to be. She sometimes worried she was becoming too dependent on him, that she was forgetting how to be alone, how to be strong without him. Then there were times like this, when just knowing he was in this with her made her stronger, not the opposite.

Someone grabbed Meagan's arm and asked her a question and she had to turn away, and when she refocused on the stage she noticed Sam had gone. He'd been concerned about Carrie, too. She'd seen it on his face.

When they were live again, it was time for the reveal. Derek called out the first safe contestant. "Tabitha." The crowd went crazy.

Carrie and Kevin joined hands, and Meagan could see Carrie's hand shaking. In that instant, Meagan knew that although this was her vision, her show, but she just wasn't sure she had it in her to get to know the contestants and see their hearts broken. She wasn't sure she could be this close to it all next season. Next season. If there even was a next season.

"And the other dancer who is safe tonight is…Carrie. Kevin you will be going home." Meagan's breath rushed past her lips, guilt twisting inside her at the relief she felt that Carrie would continue on for another week.

Poor Kevin. What did she say to him? How did she make this better? Sure, he'd been picked out of hundreds of thousands of wannabes, but the result was the same—he was still chasing a dream, and still going home. Meagan watched as Carrie, Ginger and DJ surrounded Kevin, to comfort him.

Tabitha signed audience autographs, ignoring Kevin. Meagan realized then that she didn't want Tabitha to win. She was definitely way too close to this to be objective, and she was frustrated at herself for allowing that to happen.

Hours after the broadcast had ended, Meagan was just finishing some paperwork backstage, when her cell rang. She smiled at Sam's number, knowing he, too, was probably finishing security matters for the evening.

"Hey."

"Hey, sweetheart," he said. "Listen I'm going to be a while. We've had a few complications here tonight—*nothing to worry about*. At least, not related to security. But I thought you might want to know that Carrie is still at the rehearsal studio."

"What? What's she doing there?"

"Dancing in the dark and crying."

Meagan sucked in a breath. "Oh," she expelled. "I'm going to her now."

As Meagan arrived at the dim rehearsal studio, the sound of music touched her ears. She found Carrie in the middle of the hardwood floor, in front of the shadowy mirrors, dancing her heart out. Meagan set her purse down and opened her bag, where she kept her old ballet shoes as a reminder of how easily dreams could be lost. She stared down at the worn black shoes, her throat tight as she slipped off her street shoes, and slipped on the dance shoes.

"Want some company?" Meagan asked, flipping on the light.

"Meagan," Carrie rasped, her throat thick with tears and exertion. "I just needed—"

"To rehearse and feel like you have some control of your destiny," she said. "I know. I get it." Meagan went to the sound system and switched the music. "Why don't I teach you a routine that once got me into Juilliard."

"You got into Juilliard? I thought you went to a Texas college?"

"After Juilliard," she said, confessing the small part of her life she spoke of so infrequently that sometimes, *sometimes,* she almost convinced herself it had never happened. "How about I teach you my audition piece?"

"Yes," Carrie said excitedly. "Yes, please."

And so they danced, and danced, and danced some more. And Meagan's leg hurt, and hurt some more, but she didn't stop, until they were both ready to collapse. Until Carrie broke down in tears, and Meagan with her, and they hugged.

"I don't want to go home, Meagan. I don't want to go home."

"I know, sweetie," she said. "But this show is one opportunity, just one. There are so many more. Look at Rena. She joined a Broadway show. You don't have to win to have doors open. Focus on one week at a time."

"I'm trying. I'm trying so hard. To focus, to do well. I want to do well."

"You are. You will."

The sound of a male voice clearing his throat echoed at the door, and Josh appeared in the entryway. "I'd like to offer to take Carrie to get something to eat on the way back to the house." The light in Carrie's eyes was almost instant. Josh was at least seven years older than Carrie, but Sam thought a lot of Josh, and that held weight with Meagan.

And Meagan was in pain, and afraid she wouldn't hide it well if she didn't get some distance from Carrie fairly quickly.

"I'd like that," Carrie said, before casting Meagan a hopeful, cautious look. "Unless that breaks any of my contractual rules?"

"You're safe with Josh," Meagan said, casting him a warning look. "Right, Josh?"

"Without question," Josh assured her. Carrie hugged Meagan and gathered her things.

"Turn the light out behind you," Meagan called as she switched off the music. The lights went out, and she dropped to the floor, against the mirror, pulling her knee to her chest and squeezing her eyes shut.

She knew long before he was kneeling in front of her

that Sam was there. Felt that prickling, tingling wonderful sensation, that only he could create.

"How bad?" he asked.

She bit her lip and forced her eyes open, and that was her mistake, looking into his eyes, knowing he saw everything—her pain, her defeat, her loss of a dream. Suddenly, she felt completely vulnerable. This man knew her in ways no one else did. This man could hurt her with the same deep cut that the loss of her dancing had.

He massaged her leg, like he'd done his own any number of times, and it helped the pain but somehow made her feel all the more exposed.

"How bad, sweetheart?" he prodded.

"I deal with it." It had been what he'd said to her, when she'd asked about his leg. "And don't call me that. You call me that all the time. My name is Meagan, Sam. Meagan. I need to go back to my place." She tried to get up and moaned.

"Meagan, sit." It was an order.

"No. Damn it, Sam. I'm fine. And you don't get to tell me what to do."

His broad, damnably perfect chest of his rose and fell as long, tense moments passed. "I don't deal with it. I said that because it's what guys say. Otherwise, it makes me feel weak, and it reminds me that my life changed without my permission. But it brought me here to you. And you made this place a place I want to be. I hope that maybe, just maybe, I can do that for you."

She dropped her head back, fighting tears. "I need to leave, Sam. I need to be alone."

"If you think for one minute that I'm going to let you walk out of here alone—not that I even think you can—

you're wrong. When we're back at the house, if you want me to go, I will. But not until I know you're okay."

She forced herself to stand, forced herself past the throbbing pain that grew with each passing second. "I'm fine. It comes and then it's gone."

Sam's phone beeped, and he eyed the number, then cursed. "I have to run to the office for a few minutes. Wait for me, Meagan. If this wasn't important I wouldn't even think about leaving you. Don't be stubborn and try to take off. Okay?" His phone stopped ringing.

"It's not like I'm doing any marathons," she bit out between her teeth, and he cursed, knowing she wasn't listening.

His phone started ringing again. "I have to go. Please." He slid his hand to her neck. "Wait for me." He kissed her and then took off at a fast trot to the door.

She didn't wait. She gathered her things as quickly as she could and headed for her car, and to the E.R. where she knew she had to go for that cortisone shot.

Over the course of the next three hours, Sam called her over and over, and she refused to answer. She was exhausted and it was midnight when she left the E.R. and the painkillers had kicked in.

And she knew Sam was going to know the instant she arrived. She knew he was going to be upset, that he was going to demand answers, demand to know why she didn't wait for him. Fine, then. She was going to see him. She was going to walk right into the security house and right into his bed. She was going to take charge of what happened, she was going to make sure there was no talking. Sam had too much control, and she was taking it back.

SAM PACED, CURSING THE TIMING of Sabrina's phone call. Though the call was important to Meagan in ways he was hoping to share with her very soon, it had allowed her to escape him. And he was kicking himself for not being honest with Meagan about his leg in the first place. Maybe, if he had, she'd have felt more willing to tell him about her own.

"You're wearing out the carpet," Josh said from the couch. "Seriously, man. You haven't slept in like two days. Go rest and I'll call you the minute she shows up at her place."

Sam forced himself to stop moving and scrubbed his jaw. He needed a shave, he needed sleep. Josh was right. He couldn't even think straight.

"I'll call you," Josh said, "the absolute instant she appears. We know she's okay. She answered her phone when Carrie called her."

Right. She'd answered Carrie, but not Sam, and made some excuse about visiting a friend. "Okay. Call me." He turned away. He had to face facts. Meagan had shoved him away again. Everything male inside him wanted to throw her over his shoulder, carry her off someplace, and hold her captive until she came to her senses, until she understood how much she meant to him. Until he could erase her pain.

He hit the shower and changed into shorts and a T-shirt, and was somewhat clearer headed. As long as he knew she was safe, that would have to be enough even though he wanted to go after her, he wanted to demand they talk now. To see with his own eyes that she was okay. But every logical instinct he owned told him that was a mistake. To back off, to let her come to him. Fear that she never would, though—that was killing him.

He remembered a saying his mother had always told him. "If you love something, set it free. If it comes back to you, it's yours. If it doesn't, it was never yours." He had to let go. He had to know if she'd come to him. Sam crashed on his bed and forced himself to close his eyes.

And that was when the door to his room opened and shut again.

# 23

SAM SCOOTED UP the headboard, but he didn't dare move any farther, and instinctively, he knew if he said anything, it could set off a firestorm of…he didn't know what, but it wouldn't be good.

"Undress," she ordered. And Sam knew then that this was the Meagan from the first night in the truck, the one who'd planned to use sex to put him in his place, to control him. He wondered if she even realized what she was doing. But he did. He did, and he knew he was treading some rough terrain, because he couldn't let her do that. He reached for his shirt and pulled it over his head, then made quick work of sliding his shorts and boxers down.

He lay back down against the headboard, his shaft hard and jutting forward. Her gaze raked over him, her teeth digging into her bottom lip, and it was all he could do not to reach down and wrap his hand around his cock. But it was so clear though, that she wanted complete control.

"Here I am, *Meagan*. Now what are you going to do with me?"

Her eyes lifted to his, glinted with a hint of anger. She'd told him not to call her sweetheart, and he hadn't. Though having her tell him not to had definitely hurt, once he would have laughed it off and just called her sweetheart again.

"Don't talk." She dropped her purse to the floor, and began undressing. In a matter of seconds she would be in his arms, and he would make love to her. And he'd make damn sure she knew it wasn't just sex.

He held his breath, watching as she revealed the pink sheer bra he loved so much. Her nipples, plump and rosy and beautiful, puckered at the combination of the cool air-conditioning and his hot inspection. Next came her slacks and then her thong—also pink and sexy as hell. His eyes traced her long, toned legs and settled on the tiny V he fully intended to explore with his tongue before this night was over. His cock throbbed, pulsed, demanded to be touched.

"Don't move," she said.

His gaze lifted to hers, lingering a moment on those beautiful breasts, before he said, "Whatever you say swe—Meagan."

She inhaled, her expression flickering with an instant of emotion. She didn't like that correction, and that pleased him. She sashayed toward him, but he didn't miss the slight limp. She paused at the window beside him and yanked two curtain straps free, and instantly he knew she was after total control.

He let her climb on top of him, straddle him, teasing him by settling her perfect little backside against his erection. She held up the straps. "I know you don't mind giving me control." She leaned forward, pressing her hands on the headboard, her nipples so close he could almost taste them, her breath warm near his lips. And then for just an instant, pain flickered over her features, and she turned her head, discreetly shifting her knee before turning back to him. "Isn't that right, *sweetheart?*"

The pain, her pain, did him in, and he acted on pure instinct. Sam wrapped his arms around her and slid his hand up her back to her neck. "Meagan," he whispered, the feel of her in his arms removing any reserve he'd pretended to have. "I'll let you tie me up. I'll let you do anything to me. But not if you're trying to hide from me. Not if you're using it to hide from what's real. And that's us. Us, Meagan. We're real."

"I'm not hiding," she rasped.

"Yes, you are. You are and we both know it. What happened to telling me your story?" He leaned back and looked at her. "Or creating one together?"

"Sam," she whispered, relaxing into him. "I've just dealt with this alone for so long. It's attached to a lot of pain."

He slid his hand down her arm. "That I'll share with you if you let me."

She shifted slightly, and he felt the tension ripple through her body. Sam rolled her over beneath him, settling between her legs, elbows resting beside her head. "You're in no shape to be on top or to tie me up tonight. I expect a full dominatrix routine when you're okay— including leather." His voice softened. "Sometimes you have to let someone else carry some of the burden."

She reached up and trailed her fingers along his jaw. "I'm afraid I'll forget how to be without you."

"I've already forgotten how to be without you."

Her eyes teared up. "Sam."

He kissed his name from her lips, a slow sensual kiss that deepened slowly, before becoming something far more passionate, far more wild and emotional. They clung together, tongue against tongue, body against body.

Sam slid inside her, and he felt her fear disappear, felt it fade with every touch, every kiss. He buried himself deep within her, felt the warm wet heat of her body consume him, just as she had him in every possible way. He loved this woman, he loved her with all that he was.

A slow, sweet rhythm formed. Neither of them wanted it to end, but neither could resist the build up of sensation that was leading them into a frenzy of thrusts. Their need beckoned them to get closer and closer, yet they never seemed close enough. To touch each other everywhere, yet they were never touching enough. Until finally, finally they couldn't take anymore. She held tight to him, tensing with release, her body contracting around his cock, demanding his satisfaction as she had his heart.

When they stilled, sated and relaxed, he pulled her against him, and didn't speak, finding he was holding his breath, afraid she would withdraw.

Long seconds ticked by and then she said, "I was at Juilliard. The teacher I told you about helped me get in."

Sam kept silent, afraid he'd ruin her confidence their intimacy had brought her.

"I was one of the few students to get a full scholarship, which I needed since my parents disapproved. One day during practice, I was doing a lift with another dancer, and we fell. He tripped and I tumbled and…well, my knee went in the wrong direction. I tried to recover and return to school, but I just couldn't compete at that level. So I transferred home, and gave it a whirl at the University of Texas, still dancing, still struggling with the injury. But they had a film school there, and I gravitated in that direction and ended up in news, like I told you." She laughed, but not with humor. "My parents, at least, found that choice acceptable, if far from perfect."

"That must have been hard."

"It still is," she said. "Every time I tell myself it can't hurt me anymore, it does."

"But you never stopped loving dance," he stated. "That's true passion, if I've ever seen it."

She leaned up on one elbow. "No. I never stopped loving dance which was why in Texas, it was painful to be around it and not be able to truly live it. I needed to step away from it, but nothing else interested me."

"Until that recruiter came to your school."

"It took a while," she said, "but I needed to get excited about something to keep pushing forward. And truthfully, the connections I made there allowed this show to happen. I thought I was beyond the emotions of my own failed career enough to pursue this without it affecting me, but tonight with Carrie—that tore me up. I don't know if I can come back to the show next season if I'm this close to it."

They analyzed her options, where she thought she might go. They talked. And talked. One thing kept bugging Sam, and he had to have an answer. "Why didn't you tell me about your knee before now?" he asked. "You knew about my leg."

"That's *why* I didn't tell you," she said. "You were hurt while fighting to save people's lives. I was hurt in a pair of ballerina slippers. Who am I to complain? You're a hero, Sam. You might not still be in the army, but I'm proud that you were, and that your family is."

If Sam wasn't already in love with her, it would have happened right then. His heart softened and he wrapped her in his arms and kissed her. They made love then, no hang-ups, no barriers. And Sam had no doubt that when she curled by his side and fell asleep, her walls were still down, and he intended to keep it that way. And no one, most especially Kiki, was going to take her dream from her. He would make sure of it.

SAM WOKE TO THE BEEP of a text arriving on his cell, The message was from Sabrina. Tapes that he'd gotten from an ex-studio had been given to Kiki's uncle, the network executive. The content of the tapes, which included everything from bribery to seduction, were impossible to dismiss as misunderstandings. Sam had the thumbs-up to escort Kiki off the property.

He kissed Meagan, who was so dead to the world, she didn't even move when he got up. He'd wake her with the news that she no longer had to be worried about, at least, one problem. He quickly showered and left her a note saying that he had security detail. And then Sam went to track down Kiki.

Sam knocked on the door of the mother-in-law property, and then knocked again louder. Eventually, Kiki, dressed to the hilt with model-perfect makeup, yanked open the door. Sam should have thought her sexy as hell, but there was nothing about this woman even remotely appealing to him.

Sam stepped forward, crowding her. "We need to talk. Alone."

She rolled her eyes. "Can't this wait?"

"No," he said, leaving the screen door open and following her to the kitchen. On the counter he dropped the file he'd been carrying. "Open it."

She frowned and seemed increasingly uncomfortable. After a pregnant minute of silence as she scanned the photos and documents, which held a history of her becoming a snitch for the studio.

"So. There's nothing wrong with what I do. I help separate the losers from the winners. Of course I should get paid for it."

"You mean you sabotage programs to avoid actually having to work, while still collecting the bonus your uncle offers you."

"That's insane," Kiki said. "That's enough. You can't prove anything of the sort. I'm completely innocent." She started to turn. "I'm going to call my uncle."

"He knows everything," Sam said. "There are tapes, we made a transcript. The content makes it clear that you manufacture problems to destroy people, and get paid anyway. And if that's not enough for you, I managed to catch you on tape myself. One particular call really caught my attention. You were telling your friend Jenna about how you'd decided to stay on with this show and get rid of Meagan. You'd be amazed at the places I have audio hooked up." He motioned to the room. "Like right here in your favorite place to chat on the phone when Meagan's gone. And yes—it's legally recorded. You agreed to it in your contract for the show."

She burst into tears and before Sam knew her intention, she'd flung her arms around him. "Please. Please don't do this. I'll do anything. My uncle will disown me. He's my only family, he's—"

Sam tried to pry her off him. The woman must think he was a fool, that he hadn't fully investigated her. "You have three brothers, a sister and a living mother and father."

That's when he heard the footsteps on the porch, a trip, and a soft murmur of pain. Meagan. Meagan was on the porch and Kiki was plastered all over him.

MEAGAN CRINGED AT THE weakness in her knee and forced herself up the last of the porch stairs, seeking a shower and clean clothes, wondering at the screen door.

She hated so much that she'd missed Sam this morning. She'd heard him leave, and had scrambled for clothes, but couldn't catch him before as he drove away. Somehow the idea of seeing him after the intense experience of the night before, made her feel a little shy and nervous. She was never shy and nervous.

Voices sounded in the house just as she was about to push open the door. Kiki and— Meagan frowned. "Sam?"

Ridiculous butterflies fluttered in her stomach at the prospect of seeing him yet she desperately wanted to reaffirm how right last night had been, how right they were. Her steps quickened, and she froze; in fact, she was pretty sure her heart completely stopped beating. Kiki was pressed against Sam, intimately, and...

Shock came hard and fast, with the force of a concrete block. Meagan gasped and rushed away, instinct sending her into flight. She couldn't catch her breath.

She stumbled down the stairs and almost fell, but she pushed past it, righted herself and hit the beach at a limping run—forgetting her car, forgetting anything but the fastest escape. Air came in salty gulps, as she bit back a sob.

Sam's shouts followed almost instantly. "Meagan! Meagan!"

She heard him, she did, but she wanted distance, she wanted freedom. She wanted to get away. Had to get away. She ran toward the water. She had no idea why.

Suddenly, his hand gripped her arm, and he turned her toward him.

"Go away, Sam."

"Meagan." His chest rose and fell from his fast sprint. "Sweetheart."

"Don't call me that. I told you not to call me that."

"I know you don't mean that, any more than you think I want that woman. You know I don't."

She searched his face, but didn't have to look too hard. She knew there would be sincerity in his eyes, knew it in her heart. She even knew she was being silly and irrational. "I do. I do. I just…" The ache inside her wouldn't ease. This man could so easily tear her heart to shreds. How did she say that and not put herself even more at his mercy? "It's just…" She jerked away from him and stumbled backwards, her feet, shoes and all, sloshing into the water.

He followed her right into the water, boots plunging into the ocean.

"Sam, back off. Just back off. Give me time to process what I'm feeling."

He stepped closer, but she took off running.

But Sam had her arm again, forcing her to face him. "I'm not letting this go. I'm not letting *you* go."

"You have to!" she yelled, jerking away from him and stumbling backwards again. She tumbled, arms flaying as she reached for Sam and he reached for her, but it was too late. She landed on her butt, with water splashing all around her, her hair totally drenched. She glared up at Sam. "You didn't have to choose that moment to listen to me."

"I wasn't trying to." He extended a hand and pulled her to her feet. She tugged him forward, intending to stand and throw him into the water but she wasn't fast enough. He fell into the water and on top of her.

His hands braced the sand at her sides. "I'm not letting you go. Last night—"

She shoved at him. "People are watching. You're going to get me in trouble. I can't focus like this. I can't focus on the show and the ratings and—"

"Because of me."

She couldn't say yes. She tried. On some basic level, she knew he would walk away if she pushed hard enough. So why wasn't she pushing?

"You know, Meagan," he said, "I thought I could get you to open up to me. I thought after last night you had. Clearly, I was wrong. You're looking for a reason to get away from me." He shoved off of her, left her in the water, which spoke volumes to Meagan. He wasn't helping her get up. He was showing her that she was on her own now from here on out.

He stood, looking down at her, ocean slashing around his feet, around her face. "Chase your dreams, Meg. Kiki is gone, as in terminated. That's why I left you last night, to meet with Sabrina, and compile the evidence for executive approval. Kiki wanted your job and was plotting to get you fired. And I'll stop distracting you. I'll ask to be removed from the show." He turned away and headed down the beach.

Kiki was gone—but that barely registered. Sam was leaving, Sam was all but gone already. "Sam! Sam, please." She struggled to get up and damn, her knee buckled. "Sam!" Desperation rose inside her. And she knew then and there that losing Sam was far more frightening than was the fear of being hurt. She already hurt. She hurt because he was leaving, she hurt just thinking about never touching him again, never just being with him again. She couldn't let him go. "Sam." She swallowed hard, and then with resolve firmly in place, shouted, "Sam! I love you. I love you. Please don't walk away."

She couldn't go after Sam and she couldn't watch him go. She let her chin drop to her chest, staring at the water splashing around her.

But then, he was there, in the water, on his knees, too, his hands framing her face. "I love you too, sweetheart. I thought I should wait to tell you until you were ready to hear the words, until I bought you a ring and… until I thought you'd agree to marry me."

Slowly, he got to his feet and brought her up with him. He kissed her. Ahh, how he kissed her, salty and sweet, and wicked and wonderful. And when they finally stopped, and trudged through the water, his arm around her to help her walk, there was an audience, a group of cast and crew, to watch them. Neither Meagan nor Sam cared.

Sam stopped and stared into her eyes. "So? Will you marry me, Meagan Tippan?"

"Do I get to tie you up and have my way with you, if I do?"

"Only if you promise to wear leather."

"Then, yes!" she said. "I'll marry you, Samuel Kellar."

He picked her up and carried her toward the house, carrying her because he knew she was injured. And Meagan knew, she was never going to walk alone again.

# *Epilogue*

WEEKS LATER, CENTER STAGE, Derek waited with the last two contestants—Tabitha of all people, and ironically, Jensen. The final show had arrived on the announcement that there would be a second season. They were on a ratings high, even with the curse being weaned slowly into the background. A strategy Meagan had proposed to Sabrina to ensure the ratings would hold for the next season and it had paid off.

Meagan stood backstage with Carrie by her side, now her intern, after being eliminated from the competition several weeks back. Carrie was learning the ropes amazingly well, and Meagan was pretty darn certain she'd be able to justify a staff position for her next season. And since she and Josh had become a hot commodity, Carrie had an extra incentive beyond her career to make L.A. her home.

As for Meagan, this was her baby, and Sam had convinced her to stay on as well. He'd helped her see how many opportunities the show had created for all kinds of people associated with the program, even beyond the dancers. Besides, by the end of season two, he'd have his business up and running, and she could reevaluate what she wanted to do if there was a season three. She was thinking about a reality show called *Men of Kellar Security,* but Sam wasn't buying it. She'd work on that, though.

Derek opened the envelope and drew out the results, "The winner of a new Ford Mustang, a check for one hundred thousand dollars, and a two year contract with the network as featured talent is…Jensen!" Screams erupted, and Tabitha, bless her sweet little heart, stormed off the stage in true Tabitha style.

Hours after the broadcast and debut season had ended, Meagan walked onto the empty stage, smiling at the empty auditorium. Her dream had come true, in so many more ways than she'd ever believed possible.

"I thought I might find you here."

She turned with a smile to find Sam, looking gorgeously masculine, dressed in black slacks and a blue button-down that matched his sky-blue eyes to perfection.

"We have a flight to catch."

Excitement filled her. "I know. I can't wait. Italy, here we come." They'd been planning it for weeks.

He wrapped her in his arms and held out a velvet box. "Sure you don't want to see it now?"

"Not until we get there," she said, with absolute certainty. This was one area she was more than willing to give him full control over. "What if you don't like it? I really want you to have a ring you love."

"I can guarantee that I'll love it," she said. "I'll love it because I love you, and because you always surprise me in such a perfect way." She couldn't stop smiling.

"But I have a surprise for you, too." She unbuttoned the top of her blouse to reveal a glimpse of a black leather strap. His eyes glimmered with instant heat, which she planned to flame for the rest of her life.

\* \* \* \* \*

# COMING NEXT MONTH from Harlequin® Blaze™
## AVAILABLE SEPTEMBER 18, 2012

## #711 BLAZING BEDTIME STORIES, VOLUME IX
*Bedtime Stories*
### Rhonda Nelson and Karen Foley
Two of Harlequin Blaze's bestselling authors invite you to curl up in bed with their latest collection of sensual fairy tales, guaranteed to inspire sweet—and *very* sexy—dreams!

## #712 THE MIGHTY QUINNS: CAMERON
*The Mighty Quinns*
### Kate Hoffmann
Neither Cameron Quinn nor FBI agent Sophie Reyes is happy hanging out in Vulture Creek, New Mexico. But when Cameron helps Sophie on a high profile case, he realizes that sexy Sophie has stolen his heart.

## #713 OWN THE NIGHT
*Made in Montana*
### Debbi Rawlins
Jaded New Yorker Alana Richardson wants to go a little country with Blackfoot Falls sheriff Noah Calder. He just needs to figure out if she belongs in his bed...or in jail!

## #714 FEELS SO RIGHT
*Friends With Benefits*
### Isabel Sharpe
Physical therapist Demi Anderson knows she has the right job when the world's sexiest man walks into her studio, takes off his shirt and begs her to help him. Colin Russo needs Demi's healing touch...but having her hands on him is sweet torture!

## #715 LIVING THE FANTASY
### Kathy Lyons
Ali Flores has never believed in luck, until she accidentally lands a part on a video game tour. Now she's learning all about gaming. But what she *really* likes is playing with hunky company CEO Ken Johnson....

## #716 FOLLOW MY LEAD
*Stepping Up*
### Lisa Renee Jones
The host and one of the judges of TV's hottest reality dance show put the past behind them and embark on a sensually wild, emotionally charged fling!

You can find more information on upcoming Harlequin® titles, free excerpts and more at www.Harlequin.com.

HBCNM0912